A Little Bit of the Moon

Gus Duffy

Published by Dodger Ligus Publishing, 2018.

This is a work of fiction. Similarities to real people, places, or events are entirely coincidental.

A LITTLE BIT OF THE MOON

First edition. April 19, 2018.

Copyright © 2018 Gus Duffy.

Written by Gus Duffy.

Thank you to the following:

First and foremost the most beautiful woman in the world, my amazing and incredible wife Lisa. My best friend, business partner and soul mate, who has worked so tirelessly on this project and has always believed in me.

My 'boy' Leah, who is a top mate of ours and has been there 100% on this project and given so much.

Rob Jones of *Missing Andy* who has been behind this project for four years. We finally got there!
The book was inspired by the following *Missing Andy* songs:

Glorious
Slip away
River
Sort it out
Breathless
Under pressure
It's over
Trojan horse

Check out *Missing Andy* on Facebook and Twitter for more info.

A Little Bit of the Moon
Written by Gus Duffy

* * * *

'All I ever wanted was to get away, forget who we are for just another day. And all I ever wanted was to get away, but here we are, right back in the maze.'

Gus Duffy

For My Lisa

Slip Away

'LET'S SLIP AWAY, LET'S slip away, let's run away to somewhere we'll be safe'

• • • •

GLORIA'S BAR, SOUTHERN Spain

"OK guys two truths, one lie." said Natasha in her usual cheerful way.

"Ooh, that sounds fun, how do you play that?" asked Jess excitedly.

Leah couldn't help wondering how Jess could think something sounded fun when she had no idea what it was. That was typical Jess, she was a fucking irritating hippy.

"What you have to do right," continued Natasha, "is you say three things about yourself, two are true and one is a lie and we have to guess which is a lie. I'll go first."

So far Spain had been a massive disappointment. OK Leah hadn't had a great deal of choice about the move but even so. What had she been expecting? She wasn't sure, probably the stuff you saw on the crap reality TV shows which her mum liked, *The only way is Marbs* or whatever. She thought it would be days spent on the beach sipping mojitos before going to pool parties then finishing the evening drinking expensive champagne on yachts with millionaires. Instead she was in Gloria's bar which was where they went pretty much every night.

It was a small dark, depressing bar in a dingy backstreet just outside Fuengirola, surrounded by tall buildings which blocked out what little sunlight there was in February. There wasn't even a jukebox in the bar, just a table football game which no one ever used. Leah smiled to herself as she decided that this must be how foreigners felt when they arrived in Britain after watching Mary Poppins and ended up on the Stonebridge Park Estate. The strangest thing of all though was you didn't make friends as such when you moved to Spain, not with people you'd choose to be friends with anyway. You sort of got thrown in with people so you ended up spending your time with hippies or northerners or boring people, or in Leah's case, a combination of all three.

"Number one I met Lisa Kudrow, number two I was my sister's maid of honor and number three I've got David Beckham's autograph."

Natasha was the youngest of this unusual bunch. Twenty years old and from Bolton, she was a quarter Jamaican and despite her blonde curly hair and green eyes, you could see she had slightly Caribbean features. Of course, anyone entering the bar was going to recognise her. She'd been famous since she was six years old when she'd starred in that kids sitcom *Why Always Me?* and then had all those hits as a singer, *Nat's life*, *Unfriended*, the *World In Motion* remix where she did that excruciating rap with John Barnes. She was wearing a baseball cap with 'Ibiza' written on it but she nearly always wore hats or hoods to avoid recognition, which was understandable. She'd received all that money on her eighteenth birthday and famously ended up on crack and heroin, gone into rehab, got involved with a horrible yardie, given evidence for him in his murder trial, which got him a not guilty and... Leah didn't really like to think about the rest of it too much.

Jamie smiled, "Well I know Lisa Kudrow was on your show cause my little brother used to watch it, it was on after *Drake and Josh* if I'm not mistaken? Anyway, you met her and we know for a fact you were your sister Sophie's maid of honor as you never stop going on about it. I remember Victoria Beckham was on your show but not David so I'm gonna go with that, although wasn't David Beckham in the England team when you did the song with them? I actually give up, I don't know which one is the lie."

Natasha burst out laughing, "Oh shit I messed it up. I forgot to think of a lie! I'll do it now, someone else go."

"Fucks sake Tasha it was your game, I thought you'd at least understand this one." said Taylor laughing.

"Right I'll go." said Jamie.

Leah just knew all three statements she was about to hear were bound to be boring. Jamie was thirty-one and from Exeter and... what else could you really say about him? He was boring. He had short hair and a beard and was wearing what he normally wore, shorts and a Jack Daniel's T-shirt (OK, in fairness he didn't always wear the Jack Daniel's T-shirt, sometimes he wore a Jim Beam one, or James Bond or Budweiser or Family Guy). He was much chattier in messages than he ever was in person and he had that weird habit of writing things in messages that you could never imagine him saying in real life and that really annoyed Leah. She always sort of heard the person's voice when she read a message and it took a real effort of imagination to do that with Jamie. He was possibly shy. He seemed to be much more comfortable around women than men but he wasn't gay. For one thing he was clearly head over heels in love with Taylor. Not that Taylor had any idea. Leah knew though, she could see these things, she could also see without any shadow of doubt that he was heading for disappointment there. She didn't really care though.

"Number one I can play the guitar, number two, I wasted all my money before I came here and number three I can speak fluent Chinese."

Leah didn't think she'd ever seen Jess look more impressed. "Really?" she asked excitedly "Cantonese or Mandarin?"

Leah couldn't resist, "Oh I know! Neither because that was the lie! You fucking idiot Jess."

Jess ignored Leah but looked a bit shocked, "Really? I knew you played guitar but I can't imagine you blowing all your money."

"Yeah it's a long story." said Jamie, not looking like he wished to elaborate. He half looked at Taylor who nodded as if to imply she knew the story.

"Ok, I'll go." said Taylor quickly. "Number one, I moved here to write a book on Spain."

Leah knew this was a load of bollocks. She presumably moved to Spain because her brother Dave lived here, he had been raised in Spain from a young age. When Taylor's dad had fled to Spain he'd taken Dave with him. Then he'd had to flee again this time to Northern Cyprus and Dave had stayed in Spain. He was older than Taylor of course and they had different mums but there was a reason that their dad had taken him on the run with him. Something about Dave's mum. She killed herself? Or she was in jail or maybe rehab? It was something along those lines. Leah had been told but she hadn't really been paying attention and had therefore forgotten. She remembered Jess cried about whatever it was, but that didn't really narrow it down much.

Taylor was twenty-seven and from Rochdale. Looking older than her years, she was hard faced and didn't really show any emotion. She was good-looking but quite tough looking with it, dyed blonde hair and a few tattoos. Unlike Dave she never boasted that her dad was a famous gangster. She was a single mum to three-year-old Bennie, he wasn't with her today though, she had said earlier where he was but again, Leah didn't much care so hadn't really listened. She seemed intelligent in the way she spoke (the words she used, not her Rochdale accent, all northerners sounded stupid to Leah) and she was dressed sort of sensible and mumsy yet she managed to look attractive. Leah didn't like that. Leah didn't really like Taylor at all. It wasn't that they argued it was that they were just members of the same group rather than friends in their own right. The two of them just never seemed to have clicked.

"Number two," continued Taylor, "Bennie was actually conceived in Spain. And number three I was deaf when I was a child."

Leah switched off while they discussed Taylor's answers and by the time she could be bothered to give the conversation her attention again it was Jess' turn.

Jess thought for a minute, "Ooh I've got it!" she said sounding excited.

Jess was twenty-eight years old and from Bristol and not only took absolutely no pride in her appearance, but worse than that she took pride in the fact that she took absolutely no pride in her appearance. It wasn't that she didn't have the raw material to be good-looking, it just seemed that she didn't particularly want to be. Leah felt that Jess could have been extremely pretty, God gave her the raw material and she seemed to have thrown it back in his face and committed some kind of image suicide. It would help if she would wear makeup but of course being a vegan hippy with a strong interest in animal rights, Jess never wore makeup. She was wearing a weird baggy robe thing that looked like it had been borrowed from an Ethiopian shepherd and although she spoke in a posh middle class way you could still hear her natural Bristol accent sneak out in the odd word. In spite of everything Leah quite liked Jess. True they had very different views and they clashed a lot but Leah quite enjoyed their arguments and without her Spain would have been even more boring. She wouldn't be admitting this to Jess anytime soon though.

"Number one I helped to build a school in a village on my gap year. Number two I plan to move to South America eventually, I moved here to learn the language."

Leah saw her window and quickly interrupted, "Ooh don't forget your lie Jess."

Jess looked really upset, "Leah why do you have to spoil the game?"

"I didn't!" smirked Leah trying not to laugh. "You did with your stupid obvious hippy truths."

"Leah why don't you see if you can go without saying a truth that will get you arrested." snapped Jess sounding really annoyed.

Leah decided not to participate in this boring game and instead threw peanuts into Natasha's drink, Natasha giggled and threw some back into Leah's. After the abortive attempt at playing a game, Jess spent the next ten minutes or so lecturing them all about Africa.

Leah was twenty-seven years old and from Gillingham, Kent. Although she'd been on *Question Time* and been in some of the newspapers, no one ever seemed to recognise her in Spain, which of course she was very relieved about. She was wearing a short summer dress and an expensive pair of D&G sunglasses, which used to be Natasha's, but Leah felt they suited her more so she'd borrowed them and never given them back, that was a month ago and Natasha had never mentioned it.

Leah knew she was good-looking. She kept herself fit and the fact she was half Indian meant she was permanently tanned and looked exotic. She was proud of her figure and she was proud of her face. She had dark marble eyes and she knew they made her look mysterious and sexy, she'd been told that enough. She also knew that men liked the way that she talked, she always pronounced every syllable of every word in full. Not in a posh way, Leah wasn't posh, just because she felt you should say things properly. *The Daily Mail* had said she had 'a childlike inquisitiveness and a unique way of sounding innocent when she was saying something guilty and sounding guilty when she was saying something innocent.' She liked that.

Being half white British and half Indian Leah looked Spanish. She always had done but this had been a problem since she moved to Spain, Spanish people assumed that she was Spanish and would speak to her in Spanish and when they realised she couldn't speak it they'd get frustrated with her. Leah didn't think that was fair at all, considering none of the others spoke it either. Not even Dave and he grew up there. But the point was that she felt she looked far too glamorous to hang around with this lot.

If they didn't look odd enough Taylor's brother Dave entered the bar. He probably joined them about once a week on average, Leah had no idea what he did the rest of the time as he didn't seem to have any other friends. He had a job but was quite vague about the details. A lot of expats in Spain were a bit secretive about what they did for a living because a lot of the jobs were quite dodgy, however she got the impression that in Dave's case it was far more likely that his job was perfectly legal and he was secretive as he wanted people to think he was a criminal. Dave was a bit like that. Dave was a bit odd really, he was thirty-three and had a London 'rude boi' accent for absolutely no reason and he dressed like a hip hop star from LA. He looked and sounded ridiculous. He liked to think he was a gangster and he'd happily claim he was 'running his dad's Spanish operations' but it was clearly wishful thinking. Leah suspected that it was far more likely that Taylor had been entrusted with that particular job. He liked to refer to himself as 'Stone Cold' which of course was his dad's nickname but no one else except Dave himself, ever called Dave 'Stone Cold'. When he was with them Leah felt they looked even more odd as a group than usual. He was likeable though.

Jess continued with her lecture, "It's called transgenerational trauma."

Everyone looked confused except ironically Dave who gave Jess a nod and smile of recognition, "Yeah like it is like, confusing for the older generation when dey see trans people and dey find out like, dat birds got a cock or whatever, dey aint really used to it ya know, dey can get traumatised innit."

Jess smiled patiently, "That's not exactly what it means Dave. It's not old people getting confused about transsexuals, transgenerational trauma is where something so horrific gets inflicted on one generation that subsequent generations still feel the effects and as a consequence are disadvantaged. Although I do agree with you that the elderly tend to struggle with the concept of transexuality."

At this point Jamie's cousin Gloria, whose bar they were in, arrived with a tray of drinks and looked confused.

"Jess was just telling us where a lot of Africa's problems stem from." explained Jamie.

But before she could explain Dave did it for her, not exactly in the words Jess had just used, he, well he summed up, nodding wisely he said, "Africa has bare problems ya know!"

Leah thought moving to Spain would be more glamorous than this.

Part 1

THE RIVER: LEAH

'She Lived By The River Don't You Know? She Only Had Two Ways To Go.'

Chapter 1

TWELVE MONTHS AGO, Gillingham, Kent

It was about a year ago when it all changed. It seemed like much longer now. It was long before she met Jess or Natasha or Jamie or Taylor or any of them. She'd never even heard of Fuengirola then. Leah still lived at home which was a tiny council flat in a tower block in Gillingham. It was just her and her mum who lived there yet it still felt small. Her mum was sixteen years older than Leah and looked exactly how Leah would look if she was sixteen years older and white.

The night everything changed Leah and her mum were watching the news on the sofa in their living room. Actually that wasn't true, they weren't watching the news as such, it was on after the rubbish reality show which Leah's mum insisted on watching and neither of them could be bothered to change the channel. Leah wasn't really concentrating till he appeared on the screen. She couldn't breathe for a second. Looking at that ugly, horrible cunt's face brought it all rushing back. She felt like she'd been stabbed with something which was leaking fear into her. It was as if she'd been injected with terror and she could feel it rushing round her, consuming her. Just looking at that picture of him made her feel weak, and stupid, and powerless and frightened.

Then she heard the words the newsreader was saying.

"Iqbal Hussein who was cleared of rape and robbery charges was stabbed to death outside the Regal kebab house where he worked after locking up the takeaway at around 3:15 am last Saturday. The National Retaliation Force or NRF, which is widely believed to be a cover name for right-wing protest group Action Five-Sixteen, has claimed responsibility for the attack. We now go over to our correspondent Donald North. Donald? Is the NRF really a separate organisation?"

The Donald guy was standing outside the Regal kebab shop which was only ten minutes down the road from Leah's estate. Leah listened intently.

"In all probability Nigel, no it isn't. Scotland Yard for example, have said there is absolutely no evidence whatsoever to suggest that the group even exists. However, as long as it continues to claim responsibility for attacks which are suspected of being carried out by Action Five-Sixteen, then Action Five-Sixteen will be able to remain a legal, although highly controversial organisation. But one of the most worrying developments as far the government are concerned is the recent survey which revealed that 92% of Action Five-Sixteen supporters would continue to support the group even if it transpired that the National Retaliation Force was just a cov-"

The screen went blank and Leah was still so shocked by what she'd just watched that it took her a few seconds to realise that her mum had switched it off. "What did you turn it off for?"

"It's over now Leah." said her mum, with an air of authority that didn't suit her.

"No it isn't! He was halfway through a sentence! Put it back on!"

Her mum didn't put it back on. Instead she got up and held Leah's arm, she turned it to reveal the set of recent horizontal scars.

"No Leah. I mean *this* is over." She slightly slurred the words, great, she was pissed again.

Her mum was so annoying when she was pissed, which had been every night recently. Leah knew that if a blind person lived in their flat then it would be obvious to said blind person that a single mother who'd had her only child very young, lived in the flat with her daughter who was clearly a waste of space, off the rails and a cause for concern. What wouldn't be obvious though, Leah felt, was which one of them was which.

Her mum carried on slurring and muttering away. Leah didn't really bother to listen, what was the point in listening to someone who wouldn't even remember what they'd said by the morning?

She did hear her mum say something to Leah about how she'd got justice now. That made Leah really angry, really fucking angry.

"Justice?! They didn't even prosecute him for what he did to me. Never mind his three pervert friends. And they let him off for what he did to those other girls. *They let him off.*"

She wouldn't ever forget the day she reported it to the police. The woman who examined and interviewed her had been all polite and full of false sympathy but none of them really gave a fuck. They'd picked her statement apart. Yes she was drunk at the time. No she couldn't remember every single detail. Yes she'd accepted cocaine and alcohol from Hussein on that night and other occasions. No she didn't know who the other three men were. Yes she'd voluntarily gone to a flat with them where she'd taken cocaine and consumed alcohol. No she didn't recall the exact location of the flat. No there were no independent witnesses. Yes she'd left it two weeks before reporting it. Yes she'd since showered. Yes she'd since washed her clothes.

Then it was, 'We *do* believe you. We just need to be straight with you about how this works... When the CPS take all these factors into account... No forensic evidence... Your word against his... Unlikely to result in a conviction.' Then while she was waiting for the policewoman she'd been talking with to get her a cup of coffee she'd noticed one of the coppers from the front desk staring at her tits.

Action Five-Sixteen obviously hadn't let him off though. Action Five-Sixteen were Leah's police.

The terror she'd felt when she'd first seen him on the news had gone but she still felt the same intensity of emotion, only now she felt lots of different things. She wondered if they'd laughed at him as he was scared and helpless. She wondered if he'd tried to fight them off but been overpowered and realised there was absolutely nothing he could do to stop them. She wondered if they'd spat on him. She hoped so.

When Leah was little and went round to a friend's house the other child's parents would always say what a polite young lady Leah was, how she always said please and thank-you. It was true. Leah put her coat on and walked towards the front door.

"Where are you going?" Leah could see that her mum was trying to focus as she asked this.

"To thank my police."

Her mum shook her head and rolled her eyes. "Stay away from those people Leah, they're trouble."

Leah knew there was no point in arguing. Not with her mum already this pissed, but she was fired up now and couldn't stop herself. "At least they obviously believed me! You didn't."

"Leah that's not fair!"

"No. You're right. You did believe me. You just didn't care."

Her mum stood up and screamed, "Leah of course I bloody care!"

"No you don't. You just get needy and clingy to me when you're single. I can always tell when you're single by the way. Not just because you get even more pathetic than usual. But because when you do have a boyfriend, the fridge is always full of cans of super tenants."

Now her mum was angry too. "Why are you such a spiteful cow Leah?"

Leah looked up at the ceiling and pretended to think, she then looked at her mum. "Mmm. Not sure. Could be nature or nurture really couldn't it? Why don't you open another bottle of Lambrini and watch some more reality TV? You're good at that."

As Leah opened the front door her mum yelled after her that she was, and always had been an attention seeking drama queen. Leah smiled. "Oh dear, that's a shame. I'd hoped I was adopted. But I obviously take after my mother." Then she walked out and slammed the door.

Chapter 2

AS SOON AS SHE'D LEFT the flat she'd googled Action Five-Sixteen. According to most reports the leader was a guy called Jason Skilton who was from South East London although there was no reference to him whatsoever on the official website. The website had a contact link and Leah had messaged 'Thankyou for keeping us safe. From a grateful citizen.'

She would have left it there but within minutes she got a Facebook message from Darren Wyndham who she'd been at school with. Darren was one of the Gillingham hooligan firm, and from what she'd seen on the Action Five-Sixteen website, it would make sense that he'd be a member. It seemed that the organisation was mainly made up of football hooligans. Leah and Darren hadn't spoken since school, but he asked her to come straight to the Action Five-Sixteen head office in an hour to meet the leader of the movement and sent her the address.

The office was above a shop. It was tiny and just had a desk and two chairs but no other furniture. On the wall there was a large Union Jack and a framed photo of a strict looking man with a moustache. Standing behind the desk was Jason Skilton who was aged about thirty-five and looked hard. He had a good-looking face with a slightly broken nose, high cheekbones and dark hair with a few greyish streaks which was cropped very short. He had greenish brown eyes which Leah later noticed would go quite green and bright and almost light up when he was excited and talking passionately and would go dark brown when he was quietly thinking or brooding and a strange greeny grey colour when he was angry. He was around five foot eleven and was average build but you could see he preferred drinking lager to going to the gym. He was wearing blue jeans and Adidas trainers, an Aquascutum check scarf and a black jacket which was done up. Next to his right eye he had a few scars which looked old and very faded so you could only really notice them in the light. Leah thought that he kind of looked like the 'tough' one that most boy bands have, who does pretty much nothing but raps on some of the songs which never get released and are just used to fill up the album.

"Pleased to meet you Leah. Your profile pic don't do you justice kid."

Leah wasn't really sure what to say to that. She looked away from Jason to the picture of the cross looking man. When Leah was little she'd been shy and when she felt shy or awkward she'd ask questions. She'd never lost that habit and would still instinctively ask questions. An ex boyfriend once told her that she sounded like a five-year old on a car journey and she knew it was true but she couldn't really help it. She felt a bit awkward now and she also wondered who the cross looking man was. "Who is that man?"

Jason looked at the portrait then back at Leah. She noticed that he had a way of looking into your eyes and suppressing a smile which could make it feel like he didn't like you and had noticed someone sneaking up behind you with an axe.

"That's Enoch Powell. He's the one who predicted all this. We take our name from him, Action cause we don't just sit on out arses, and five-sixteen cause E is the 5th letter of the alphabet and P is the 16th. We don't make a personality cult of him though. As far as we're concerned he weren't a genius, he just spoke the plain fucking truth. Let me ask you something, what is it you think I do Leah?"

Leah thought for a moment. She decided it was best not to say that she strongly suspected that he organised the murders of black and Asian men who were suspected of being criminals. She'd better say something different, what did she see on their website? "You're uniting all the hooligans?"

"No Leah I'm not. That's been tried before and it doesn't work. The U.K's football casuals don't *want* to unite, they want to compete, that's how it works. They can't even unite for a whole World Cup, Mackems won't drink with Geordies, Wednesday and the Blades Business Crew won't even look at each other and as for Portsmouth and Southampton..." he trailed off.

Leah had absolutely no idea what he was on about. Wednesday? What was happening on Wednesday? But Jason continued.

"Well let's put it this way, you're absolutely gorgeous Leah and I could put you on our website and say, 'Leah wants us to unite!' And for five minutes they would, then five minutes later they'd be throwing chairs at each other again.

But if I said, 'The lovely Leah will be wearing a football strip on our website next month. But which one? It's up to you lads. Whoever Leah feels has been the top Action Five-Sixteen division wins!'

All of a sudden, Millwall would go on the absolute rampage, then Tottenham, then Chelsea, then West Ham... You see what I mean? You'd become a trophy."

"I'd like to be a trophy!" She meant it too.

"I think you could be more than that. Let me ask you a question and answer it honestly. What do you think of slavery?"

Jason had a way of answering what she'd said and then asking a question that wasn't really connected to it. This felt like a cross between a first date and a job interview. She also noticed that he asked her permission to ask her questions, which made what he was saying seem more important somehow.

Leah thought she knew what Jason wanted to hear. It wasn't that bad... They had a shit life in Africa anyway... It didn't even happen and was all a hoax... Something along those lines, but he said to answer honestly so she did.

"Honestly? I'm sorry but I think it was absolutely disgusting."

"You're wrong Leah. It wasn't disgusting, it *is* disgusting. Did you know there are currently more slaves now than there have ever been at any point in history? The vast majority of whom are black Africans."

"Really?"

"Google it. You see, leftists don't give a fuck how black people get treated, they only care how white people treat them. This is because they believe the white man is biologically racially superior, and therefore morally more responsible. We on the other hand believe the British are culturally superior regardless of the colour. Do you see how it's the leftists who are the *real* racists?"

"Someone should tell the world this!"

Jason had a strange way of looking at her. He seemed fascinated by her. No one had ever looked at her in that way before. It wasn't that he fancied her (although he obviously did) it was more the way someone looks at a new phone or car or something they're about to buy and gets more and more excited as they see all the different apps or gadgets or things that it does.

"Yes Leah they should."

"Why don't you?"

"I have a broken nose, convictions for racist violence and a Stone Island jacket. I'm not convinced they'd listen to me."

"You could take the coat off and wear a suit and tie."

Jason nodded and Leah could see he was trying not to laugh.

"Good point Leah. I hadn't thought of that, but I might still have the broken nose and convictions for racially aggravated criminal damage and assault."

Leah felt a bit silly."Good point."

"They need to hear it from someone more elegant than me. You're the one we've been waiting for Leah."

There was something Leah felt she'd better say. She felt embarrassed as she said it, it felt like a confession.

"You know I'm half Indian right? Well my dad was Indian but I never met him and he died. My mum found out he was dead when I was six but I wasn't sad cause I didn't know him, but I cried, cause you're supposed to aren't you? But basically I'm half Indian."

Jason probably thought she was Spanish. People always thought she was Spanish, and she'd never even been to Spain! But he didn't look in the least bit surprised when she told him. In fact he looked delighted.

"You can't be half from a country Leah. Half your family are Indian. Half mine are Irish. I had to make a choice what culture I was, just like you. And just like you Leah I'm British. We both made the right choice. You hungry by the way? I'm quite peckish. Let's go for a pizza."

Chapter 3

ONE YEAR LATER, GLORIA´S bar, Spain

"So you think it's OK?" asked Jess sounding annoyed.

"That´s not what I'm saying at all. I just meant imagine they went to Fred West´s house for example." answered Taylor.

Leah had no idea what had brought them to this point as she'd stopped listening to the conversation when Jess had started ranting to them about Africa again. She couldn't be bothered to concentrate on this rubbish anymore. This was getting really boring.

Leah had always liked TV shows about prisons, *Orange Is the New Black*, *Oz*, some other one she couldn't remember the name of, what was it? That was going to really bug her. Anyway, those programmes, she realised, worked because prison gave the writers a reason to have all these characters from totally different backgrounds all mixed in together. You couldn't do that with other shows. If for example Joey and Chandler from *Friends* started hanging out with some Mexican gang member called like, *Bone Thug* or something, then it wouldn't work. Ross would say something sarcastic, probably Leah reckoned something like 'Hey Bone Thug, you know how you call everyone essay? Well my students just wrote an essay.' And everyone would laugh, and Bone Thug would get the hump, and shoot Ross in the leg which would ruin the show. And no one would understand why Bone Thug hung around with these middle class Americans anyway.

Prison on the other hand, well, doesn't matter who you are or what environment you're from, one bad move and you're there, lumped in with all sorts. The only thing you've all got in common being the fact that you've ended up there cause of the fuck ups you've made. Leah looked at Jess, Jamie, Taylor, Natasha, and herself and realised that for expats Spain was a lot like that.

Jess was still rambling on, she was doing her patronising face today, most posh leftists had that look in Leah's experience, it seemed those who don't discriminate against anyone seem to always assume that anyone who didn't go to uni must be a thicko. And as no one at the table except Jess had been to uni, they were obviously all morons.

"Of course I don't agree with it, I'm not saying that. I'm just saying that statistically at least *one* of them must have enjoyed it!" Taylor looked deadly serious as she said this but Leah knew straight away that she was simply winding Jess up. You didn't need to have heard the conversation to know that, Taylor had that mischief look in her eyes.

She never showed much emotion but you could tell when she was on a wind up. Jess however, couldn't tell which was probably why Taylor couldn't resist doing it. It wasn't as if Taylor had any strong political opinions of her own, as far as Leah was aware Taylor had no political views whatsoever and she'd snipe just as readily at Leah if she could but Leah knew when she was she was being wound up and usually wouldn't bite which made it less amusing for Taylor so Jess copped it more.

"Would you enjoy it?" Jess looked really upset as she asked this.

The question was clearly rhetorical, and everyone else at the table looked pretty appalled by whatever Taylor had said. Leah could see that Taylor was trying not to smile.

"No. But lots of people do things I wouldn't enjoy. I wouldn't enjoy playing rugby or going to a Jedward concert or watching a subtitled Japanese film but some people do."

Jess just shook her head and Natasha piped up with, "We're talking about rape here not sports and music!"

Right on cue Jamie's cousin Gloria arrived with a tray of drinks and looked suitably horrified.

"Jess was just telling us what happens in the Congo" explained Jamie.

Jess had gone from being upset back to patronising, (Gloria hadn't been to university either.) "I was explaining how some rebel militias force fathers to have sex with their own daughters at gunpoint and therefore completely destabilise entire families and communities but you know, according to Taylor it's not so bad."

Wow. Taylor had really got a reaction here. "That's not what I said! OK, how many people has this happened to?"

"Thousands."

"Exactly! I don't know the child abuse statistics but let's say one in a thousand blokes are pedophiles and you make a thousand guys knob their kids, you've made one pedo's dream come true. That's all I'm saying."

Jamie pointed out that he could sort of see Taylor's point and that seemed to diffuse things. It was so pathetic. You could work out pretty much the entire group from this conversation. Jess getting herself worked up into a state about some weird African country that quite frankly was none of her business. Taylor winding her up yet only really making herself laugh with it. Jamie trying desperately to show that him and Taylor agreed on something, even though she was joking and he hadn't noticed. Jess stopping the rant not because someone had proved what she said was nonsense, but because Jamie had agreed with Taylor and Jess didn't want him to think that they had different views, even though he'd only agreed with Taylor in the first place so Taylor wouldn't think her and him had different views. And they weren't even Taylor's views anyway! Natasha, nodding along and chiming in with the odd comment but pretty much lost and just waiting for the conversation to move on to a subject she knew something about so she could join in, and Dave, fuck knows. Who knew what was going on in his head? Probably he was thinking of a rap song.

"Why isn't this on the news more Jess?" Jamie asked.

"Because Jamie, it's happening to black Africans so no one cares."

Maybe it was the sincerity in her voice, maybe it was the way the patronising tone cranked up a notch and her eyes bulged as she spoke. Or maybe it was the way she sort of looked at Leah just before she said it. But whatever it was, Leah retaliated.

"What a load of bollocks! If the Ku Klux Klan in Mississippi were forcing African-Americans to shag their own kids it would be all over the news! It's not cause Africans are the *victims* that no one cares. It's cause Africans are the *perpetrators*! The leftist media don't want to admit that African culture has failed compared to Western capitalism."

Jess exploded back. "Well it's the white Western companies plundering all the minerals which causes all this, so actually Leah capitalism is a major perpetrator, that along with the imbalance and disadvantage which resulted from colonisation has led to this!"

The two of them glared at each other. Then Jamie as usual tried to calm them both down,

"I thought we agreed not to talk about politics anymore after last time."

Jess sighed and sort of half smiled like someone who has to explain something to a bunch of idiots and is trying to be patient with them.

"It's not politics, it's knowledge of the world." she said it like a nursery teacher explaining to a three old that he didn't need to put on his PE kit to learn shapes and numbers.

Leah retaliated again. "Bollocks! It's you saying a communist opinion, then when I prove you're chatting bullshit, all of a sudden it's politics."

Jess kept the nursery teacher tone. "No Leah, its knowledge of the world. Then you say something racist, then Taylor says something sick. It's the same as most of our conversations."

Natasha burst out laughing. "That's so true man!"

Taylor chuckled. "I was just saying that if they turned up at Fred West's house..."

As she trailed off Dave interrupted with his own views on modern warfare. "You see me yeah? I could get bare man to do bad tings, but I don't wanna diss people like dat."

"Who's bear man?" asked Jamie. Natasha giggled and Taylor shot Jamie a disapproving look.

Dave ignored the interruption and carried on. "Besides, I'm gonna blow up as a rapper this year bwoy!"

Jamie took this opportunity to quickly undo any harm his snipe had done. Not with Dave of course but with Taylor, "Yeah definitely. How's the rap going by the way?"

This was so cringe. Everyone at the table knew how the rap was going without needing to hear it. It was going shit. All Dave's rap songs were shit. This one had started shit and would finish shit. That's how it was going.

It wasn't that Leah hated him rapping, she actually quite enjoyed it. It was pretty funny and it always made Natasha laugh which seemed to take her mind off things. What annoyed Leah was how feeble Jamie was. Pretending he cared. For one thing Jamie didn't like rap music. But even if he did, it's massively unlikely he would have liked Dave's. For another thing, Jamie and Dave didn't even like each other. Jamie humoured him, not as Leah and the others did because Dave was a sweet-natured lost soul, but because he wanted to get in Taylor's pants.

What was strange though, was how Dave hated Jamie. As far as Leah was aware nothing was or had ever gone on between Jamie and Taylor and yet Dave seemed to regard him with the suspicion of a child who's recently divorced mother is suddenly bringing her 'friend' round to meet him and he's decided to show this idiot that they come as a package and that there's no way in with him and he'll expose this moron every chance he gets. And when his real dad picks him up on Saturday mornings he'll be angelic and show what a great family they could be if only this wanker would fuck off and leave them alone to be happy. And then the stepdad gets wound up and starts to snipe back and in doing so sort of blows his cover and the mum sides with her son and it's all over.

The real dad in question was Dennis. He wasn't Dave's dad of course, he wasn't even Bennie's dad. He was Taylor's ex and he'd recently arrived in Spain to try and get back with her. Taylor had explained to the group how and why her and Dennis broke up but Leah couldn't remember the story as she had stopped listening almost immediately. Not because she wasn't interested, but because she'd got the distinct impression she was being lied to.

Leah liked Dennis. For one thing he usually paid for all their drinks. (Not that Leah had paid for a drink since she'd lived in Spain but even so.) He had only been there a matter of weeks and already he'd landed himself a job selling property investments and was earning a fortune. He was one of life's winners. If Leah was honest with herself then she had to admit that when she first met Dennis she thought she was probably going to shag him. There was something about him, he was always smartly dressed, usually in a suit and he was always well groomed, his hair was slick in a side parting and he was clean-shaven. He had a jagged scar on his cheek which looked cool but didn't really suit him.

Leah's ex, well sort of ex, Jason Skilton for example had a broken nose but he wouldn't have looked right without it. He was a thug and he was aggressive. Dennis wasn't either of those things. He was just a nice, likeable bloke. Jamie didn't seem to like him, but that didn't surprise Leah in the least. Leah had tried to flirt a bit, subtly of course, but she'd got nowhere so had given up. Dennis only ever seemed to see Taylor. It was like everyone else was... not invisible as such, cause he paid them all attention, Leah included. It was more like everyone else was a man to him and Taylor was the only woman in the world.

Ever since Leah was old enough to remember, boys had always fancied her. True Jamie wasn't interested in her but that didn't count, he was probably scared of her and anyway nerdy guys weren't her type but the Dennis situation was unique. She wouldn't be trying with him anymore, she wasn't going to embarrass herself.

She knew it wasn't personal though, he was clearly obsessed with Taylor, even though he got nothing back. In fact Taylor seemed to talk through gritted teeth when he was there, not just to him but to all of them. And still he carried on, even though he got no encouragement. Now Leah thought about it that was a bit strange. Before she could analyse it any further though Dave stood up and launched into his rap.

"I'm runnin' my old man's Spanish operation.

Whilst tryin' to hold up my family's dark reputation.

Look in my eyes, and you'll believe what you're told.

Look in my heart, see why they call me Stone Cold.

I ain't the type to scream and shout,

But man if a man look at me funny, I will take dat man out."

Natasha broke the awkward silence. "That was... Beautiful."

Dave was as good at detecting sarcasm as he was at rapping.

"Safe!" he yelled with a smile, holding his fist out for Natasha to fist bump him, which she did. Natasha's opinion on his music understandably meant a lot to him.

"Where would you take him?"

As Jamie asked this Taylor chuckled, she only intervened if Dave was upset or Jamie was making him look particularly stupid. Safe in the knowledge that he hadn't upset Taylor, Jamie continued.

"You said you'd take the man out but where would you take him? There's a place in Fish Alley that does a set menu for twenty Euros. Three courses including lobster. It's really romantic, you should take him there."

"Not take him out like that ya gherkin! I mean shoot him, innit."

"From behind?"

Dave looked annoyed and did his best threatening face. "Do you wanna get smoked homey?"

"Yeah I haven't eaten yet and I'm starving! I'm up for getting a bit of smoked homey, I've never had it before, is it nice?"

Natasha spat her drink onto the floor laughing, she was in hysterics.

Dave kissed his teeth and called Jamie a 'batty chief' which should have ended the conversation but for absolutely no reason Jess came out with, "I'll never understand why chief is used as insult. In Native American communities chief is the leader!" She did the inverted commas thing with her hands when she said 'chief' but even more annoying was the way her voice rose into a high pitch as she said the word 'leader' she pretty much squawked that word out and her eyes bulged to the extent that Leah was worried they were going to fly out of her head and land in her vodka.

Before she could stop herself, Leah retaliated. "Native American? Really?"

Jess's eyes stayed bulged. Leah put her hand over her vodka, just in case. "Yes Leah Native American or would you rather I call them Indians?"

Taylor burst out laughing. "Hardly! She doesn't like being called that herself!"

Jamie over laughed at this and Leah ignoring the snipe, shook her head and muttered the word 'cringe' which was intended to show Jamie how pathetic he was. It worked. Jamie went red and looked uncomfortable.

Leah carried on. "So a red Indian is a Native American because he was there first and we should respect his culture? And an Aborigine is a native Australian because he was there first and we should respect his culture too? Yet when I talk about native Brits and our culture being respected you call me a racist. Have a word Jess. You really put the hippy in hypocrite."

Jess didn't like that one bit. "Leah in case you've forgotten, you're an immigrant! You moved to Spain! You really put the hypocrite in hypocritical immigrant who's called Leah!"

Jamie over laughed again, this time to compensate for his over laughter at Taylor's joke. Jess however seemed to read too much into it and had a strange grin. Poor cow. Leah had noticed recently that Jess had a thing for Jamie. That was typical of Jess, she wasn't the sort of person who'd get a crush, she was the sort who'd develop feelings over a period of time. The sad thing of course was all her and Jamie really had in common was they were both heading for humiliation and heartbreak. Leah felt sorry for her.

Leah's sympathy for Jess didn't stop her wanting to use her expensively manicured nails to rip her own skin off and throw it at Jess though. She decided to wipe the silly grin off her silly face instead.

"I thought hippies were supposed to care about other people's opinions. But you discriminate against me for my beliefs! You're a fascist!" Leah smiled as she said it, she knew Jess hated being called that.

"They're not *your* opinions though are they? You're just repeating what you've been taught. I could teach my pet parrot political statements and he'd repeat them but they wouldn't be *his* views!"

She actually did have a pet parrot. He was called Mr. Miyagi. She brought him to the bar occasionally but hadn't done so since Leah had remarked that the poor bird had been colonised, snatched from his home in Africa and forced into captivity. In fact Jess hadn't mentioned Mr. Miyagi since that.

Whenever Jess was losing the argument she always brought it back to the idea that Leah's views weren't her own, that she was brainwashed by Jason Skilton. That way Jess could sort of change the subject and not have to answer the original point which Leah had made. Usually at this point Leah would tell Jess that it was strange that she was a feminist when she felt a woman could be so easily manipulated by a man. Or how Leah had appeared on *Question Time*, debated with elected MPs and been written about by the newspapers, whereas all Jess had ever done was attend some street protests, and therefore wasn't in Leah's league. But she couldn't be bothered to keep having the same conversation, so she simply told Jess that she was a patronising cow and that she didn't know or understand the first thing about Leah's opinions.

Annoyingly Jess agreed and said she only got statements from Leah which were available to any idiot on the Action Five-Sixteen website. Then she looked at Leah with sympathy which Leah noted was far more irritating than the usual big eyed patronising look but just as patronising if you thought about it.

"I'd love to know your *real* views Leah." she said softly.

Chapter 4

SIX MONTHS AGO, GILLINGHAM, Kent

Leah was buzzing! She couldn't stop smiling. Just twenty-four hours ago she'd been on *Question time* on TV. On TV! She was worried she was going to say something silly but she hadn't. She was sure she hadn't. Jason had briefed her before she went. The Left were supposed to be sending this woman who said crazy things about America and how Britain should declare war on them and Leah had some great attacks planned, but Jason had said it was a bluff, that they wouldn't send that loony woman at all, they'd send someone else at the last minute. He was right. Jason was always right.

A lot had changed in the last six months. For a start things were much better at home now. On reflection Leah felt that the main problem had been that her mum was in charge and hadn't been very good at it. She'd led them from one crises to the next, her idiot drunken boyfriends, the time she shagged that Keith guy who lived two floors up and his fiancé had painted 'slut' on their front door. Now Leah was so much more confident, she'd taken charge. It wasn't like they'd sat down and agreed this of course. It was subtle. But since Leah had started to feel so much more powerful she'd become the driving force. When everything had happened with the police and stuff Leah had hated her mum, but now she could look back and see that it wasn't as she'd thought, it wasn't that her mum didn't care, it was that she couldn't cope, she didn't know how to deal with it so had hoped it would all go away or resolve itself. Leah was different. She was tough and she now felt a bit sorry for her mum. She knew how it felt to be powerless and overwhelmed, it wasn't much fun. Now she had power she could really enjoy herself. Power was an incredible drug. She felt drunk on it.

She'd become the spokeswoman for Action Five-Sixteen which of course was a legal street protest movement. She had learned that pretty much every football mob in the country had an Action Five-Sixteen division which all competed with each other. Beating up local street gangs for example or disrupting local events which they deemed 'unsavoury' and within most divisions was an NRF unit, a very small, secretive group which did, well, the more important stuff.

She did a regular video blog on the Action Five-Sixteen website and there were T-shirts with her image on which were selling quite well. (An image of her face had even been on an England flag at a recent friendly abroad!) She'd been interviewed by newspapers and she received emails from all over the world. True some of the emails were very creepy, true some idiot kept editing her video blogs to make out she was talking dirty and putting it on YouTube, he'd already done it with her *Question Time* appearance, which was annoying. And true there was a chant that the Action Five-Sixteen lads sung on protests which said something about *'we all drink beer and we've all shagged Leah.'* But she didn't really mind that, it was just banter and they were all very kind and extremely protective over her. When Gillingham had played Brentford at home, the Brentford Division had messaged Gillingham's firm and said they weren't coming for trouble, they just wanted to meet Leah. She'd gone along to meet them at a pub in town and they'd taken a photo with her holding a Brentford Action Five-Sixteen flag. One of them, a big thuggish guy called Marris kept telling her that he wanted to marry her, while a mixed race guy in their ranks called JT told her he was considering getting a tattoo of her and asked if she'd mind!

She felt superhuman. She hadn't cut herself for months. And Jason was right, she was more than just a trophy.

Jason still hadn't made a move on her but they saw each other pretty much every day and were very flirty with each other. Leah felt like he had too much respect for her to try it on yet. She couldn't recall ever feeling as confident as she did now and no one had ever made her feel as sexy as Jason did.

She swaggered into the office feeling as high as a kite. She couldn't remember ever feeling so happy. Jason seemed to be buzzing just as much as her, maybe even more so. Leah had never seen him so excited.

"Leah you were fucking brilliant kid! Our support has gone off the wall! Have you seen how many likes our Facebook page has got?"

"It was so much fun! You were right, they *did* send someone different and not the woman they'd said they were going to send, but it made no difference, I destroyed him!"

"I loved it when you said, '*Nelson Mandela fought for the indigenous people of South Africa to run their own country rather than have a foreign culture forced on them, will you condemn him? Or just Action Five- Sixteen for trying to do the* same thing here in Britain?' And he went, '*I'm not prepared to answer that question.*' And everyone booed!"

"What about when I said, '*For a man who loves multiculturalism you don't seem to be very diverse yourself, I bet I have more ethnic minorities on my Facebook than you do in your wine tasting club!*'"

"Yeah that was great. My personal favorite was when he'd referred to you as an Asian woman three times and you went, '*Why do you keep referring to me as Asian when I'm British then calling ME racist? Can you not see me as a British woman just because I've got dark skin? You're a racist old man!*'"

"Yeah but did you see that idiot's made a clip on YouTube where he's edited it to make out like I'm talking about sucking willies? That's pissed me off."

"Yeah I saw it. In all fairness it is quite funny. Anyway you've got a million hits on YouTube and comments from all around the world. That's what counts. And one of the newspapers have done a huge double page spread on us with the headline: '*Five* examples where Leah was right, and *sixteen* reasons why the British public need *action*!'"

"Did we make the front page?"

"Unfortunately not kid because of this."

Jason handed Leah a copy of the paper. The headline said 'Nat's how you get away with murder.' The photo showed a young black man outside court sticking his middle finger up at the camera. Natasha was being helped into a car, she had a coat over her head to cover her face and was being pursued by paparazzi. The article went on to say how a notorious yardie called Kane 'big dread' Thomas had been acquitted two weeks ago of murdering a rival drug dealer and shooting a pregnant woman after his celebrity ex girlfriend Natasha had given evidence in his defence claiming he was with her all night on the night in question. The jury had believed her but the paper obviously didn't. By the look on Jason's face he didn't believe her either.

Leah knew who she was. She hadn't met her then of course, and she'd been too old to watch *Why Always Me?* but she knew her music and didn't like any of it. It was safe to say she wasn't a fan. In fact she didn't like Natasha at all.

"I fucking hate that annoying child! Do you remember *Unfriended*?" Leah then sang the chorus of Natasha's biggest hit, in the whiniest, most annoying voice she could.

"I was pleased to meet you

But more pleased to delete you.
We used to message every day. But now you've been blocked.
You just come up as Facebook user now, and it suits you a lot!"
Jason didn't laugh. "Yes Leah, it's very annoying."
"I'll say!" said Leah, shaking her head to emphasis just how annoying it was.
"What's more annoying is that she's lied for this Kane 'big dread' Thomas and the bastard's got away with murder. I don't give a shit about the dealer he shot, good, saves us doing it but the pregnant woman? He's going, tonight. We've had him under surveillance since the verdict and although him and Natasha claim to have split up they still meet once a week at 2am in a quiet alleyway. We're gonna do him there tonight."

Leah was annoyed. Not so much about the trial or verdict, but more about the fact that it had kept her off the front page. She felt she'd let Jason down. Well she hadn't, that annoying, spoilt, talentless northerner had.

"Fuck doing *him*! We should do her. Do the world a favour."

Jason didn't look convinced. "I don't think we can really kill a nineteen-year-old girl Leah."

"I can! And I will." As she said this she opened the desk drawer and pulled out a large knife then carried on. "Give me the location and I'll do it."

"I've already got someone to do it, and they're doing *him*. It's all arranged."

"Well you'd better un-arrange it then hadn't you?" said Leah, enjoying the feeling of power and control.

Leah could see from Jason's expression that he didn't think this was a good idea and was about to say so, so she continued.

"You always say it's about culture not race, and people can choose their culture. Well, she's obviously chosen hers. If she wants to act like a Jamaican yardie then we'll fucking treat her like one!"

Jason smiled and handed Leah a small can of C.S gas. "If she gets there first do her quick before he arrives, if he's there first, wait till he leaves then follow her, but do it in the alley either way. This rain is perfect, it'll really fuck it up for forensics. Should be quite simple, especially if she's off her nut on drugs. Ask for her autograph then quick squirt of gas in her face and stab, straight away. Don't slash or slice cause it makes a mess and doesn't do much damage, see this?" He pointed to a small notch in the blade. "That's the bit that fucks them. Twist the knife as you pull it out." He said all this quite calmly like someone explaining to their nan how to send an email. "Leave your phone here. Mobile phones are the fingerprint of our generation. Ninety-nine percent of murderers get caught cause their phone signal was right near the scene. They never tell you that in the papers of course, but it's true." Then he handed her a mobile phone.

"Details are in the messages. Use the phone to claim the attack then lose it and the knife immediately. You know the code word to claim the attack as the NRF don't you Leah?"

"Of course, it's 'The river.'"

"Good girl. Are you sure you're up for going all the way on this?"

Leah smiled seductively and slowly licked her lips.

"I'm up for going all the way with you, on this desk. I just have to kill an annoying little junkie first."

Jason smiled back at her. Looking her up and down.

"I'll clear the desk for when you get back." Then he moved in close to her so his face was almost touching hers. He looked into her eyes. "Don't stab straight into the ribs, it can snap the blade." he whispered, pushing his fingers into her ribs and gently stroking the bottom of her breast with the tip of his thumb. He moved his hand and pushed her softly above her stomach "Go in there and push upwards." As he whispered this his lips brushed hers. This was all very sexy but Leah wished he wouldn't make it all sound so complicated. She was bound to forget something.

As she walked to the door Jason called out to her. "Oi!"

"What?"

"You and me kid." He said with a wink.

Leah winked back, "You and me kid."

Chapter 5

FIVE HOURS LATER

Leah had been waiting in the alley for ages. It was cold. She'd probably be OK if the police pulled her now as she could perhaps justify carrying a weapon after she'd been recently attacked but what about after she'd used it? She'd go to prison for ages. She'd got carried away before with Jason. It was the whole power thing. At the time she was convinced she could easily do this, now she wasn't so sure. Not only that but she wasn't really dressed for this. She liked the dress she was wearing, it was expensive and she didn't want to get blood all over it and have to throw it in the bin. Also it was dark and raining and cold and she was standing in an alleyway. This wasn't very glamorous at all. She was just wondering how to get herself out of this when she heard footsteps and a figure appeared. Leah kept her hiding place and watched silently. Kane had arrived.

• • • •

TWENTY-FOUR HOURS LATER Leah was sitting back in the office trying her best to explain. She'd tried to breeze past it all matter of factly but Jason wasn't having any of it.

"I don't understand this Leah. You went off to stab her, but you let her off and shot him instead?"

"Yes. I changed my mind. A lady can change her mind you know Jason."

"The NRF don't use guns Leah."

"We do now."

"Where did you even get a gun? "

"I'm a resourceful girl. Don't underestimate me."

Jason rested his head on his hand. He looked baffled. "Leah none of this makes any fucking sense."

Leah put her hand on his arm."It makes perfect sense. You were right Jase. We can't kill a nineteen-year-old girl. But him? Fuck him. No one will care."

Jason looked a bit defeated. Leah had never seen that before. He half smiled and said, "You're right there. Our support is strong as ever and even the papers are backing us. You got this right kid. Was she there?"

"Nah. He was waiting for her, I shot him before she turned up. If she even did. Probably too busy taking drugs and writing annoying songs." Leah was done with talking about this now. She didn't want to answer any more questions on the subject. She slipped her dress off and climbed onto the desk.

He never asked her about that night again.

• • • •

ABOUT THREE MONTHS later Leah woke up to frantic banging on her front door. When she opened it Darren Wyndham burst in looking agitated.

Leah asked him what was wrong but he didn't answer. Instead he picked up the TV remote and flicked through the channels till he found the news. Leah could see he was shaking.

They watched in silence.

"Seventeen-year-old Dwayne Tompkins who represents the England under 18's football team was stabbed to death in a vicious, racist attack last night. Tompkins, who had no criminal convictions of any kind, was attacked as he walked home from football training. Twenty-seven-year-old Stephen Colley from Harrow, North West London has been charged with his murder which was claimed by the National Retaliation Force, a cover name for Action Five-Sixteen. Donald North, is this the end for Action Five-Sixteen?"

Donald was outside the Action Five-Sixteen office.

"As far as any further press or public support for the group is concerned Nigel, yes it certainly is. Several members have gone to the police and offered to give evidence against the organisation as they are so disgusted with this terrible murder of an innocent young English boy. Also, several police informers and undercover officers working within Action Five-Sixteen have confirmed the NRF was as suspected, merely a cover name. Thirty-six-year-old Jason Skilton believed to be the group's leader was arrested in a dawn raid this morning. Skilton, who has convictions for throwing a brick through a mosque window as well as racially aggravated violence dating back to 2002 has been charged with conspiracy to commit murder as well as inciting terrorism."

The words were still ringing in her ears when the picture went back to the news studio.

"Thank you Donald. Further violence has occurred in Honduras today following election results that-"

Darren switched the TV off and looked at Leah.

"We can't stay here. If we don't get nicked we'll get lynched. I've got friends in Belfast. I'm going there now. You coming?"

Leah smiled and shook her head. Darren nodded, told her to take care, and left. Leah knew exactly where she was going. She googled flights to Malaga airport which was the nearest to Fuengirola, and started packing straight away.

Chapter 6

THREE MONTHS LATER and here she was in sunny Spain, in Gloria's little bar being patronised by a hippy. Jess was clearly waiting for an answer on what Leah's real views were.

"Oh what's the point Jess? You'll only twist whatever I say with your big posh university words." That shut her up.

Dave broke the silence, "Natasha? Can I sample your vocals please?"

"Nope."

Dave looked like a child who'd just asked his mum for a McDonald's and been told he couldn't have one."Why not? You let MC Booya sample the *Unfriended* chorus what?"

Natasha, who was just taking a sip of her drink, spat it back into her glass laughing."Obviously I didn't let him man. He just did it! The track's called *Unlocked Killa* do you really think I wanted that released?"

"No offence but his version was better."

Natasha laughed again."Thanks Dave!"

Dennis entered the bar with a beaming grin and Dave jumped up to greet him."Yes Dennis! How you doing bruv?"

Dennis fist bumped him, "I'm all good Stone Cold"

Taylor looked at Dennis like she'd just caught him lying. "Stone Cold? For god's sake."

Dennis looked a bit timid and changed the subject. "Where's Bennie, Tay?"

Taylor was doing the gritted teeth thing again. "What's it got to do with you? You're not his dad."

This seemed a low blow but Dennis took it in his stride."No that's true. I still get a shock seeing you with blonde hair. It suits you though."

Natasha looked confused. "Was Taylor not blonde before?"

"Nah mate back when we was together she had dark hair."

Leah decided to put him on the spot."Which do you prefer Dennis?"

Dennis smiled and rolled his eyes."Oh mate you can't ask me that! Truth is I don't know. It's weird but if you asked me to name the two most beautiful women I'd ever seen in my life they'd both be the same person, you know?"

That was the thing about Dennis. His compliments were never generic. Whether he was talking about Taylor in a romantic way or to one of the others in a friendly way every single compliment he gave could only apply to the person he said it to. Taylor didn't look impressed though and went to the toilet. Leah got the impression she'd stay there till Dennis left the bar.

Jess looked at Dennis with interest. "Have you seen Bennie since you've been here Dennis?"

"Nah not yet mate, I think Tay don't wanna confuse him you know?"

Leah noticed that Dennis often asked a rhetorical question at the end of a statement.

Jess nodded."Of course. And Taylor was pregnant when you guys met?"

"Yeah bit weird ain't it? At first I was a bit funny about it, her kid with another bloke. But when we split I found I missed him as much as I missed her. Anyway, I'm only passing on my way home so I'm gonna shoot off. Great seeing you lot."

He went to the bar drank a quick shot while talking to Gloria, then left.

Taylor came out the toilet and sat back down. Natasha smiled at her. "Taylor you well shouldn't have broke up with him man." she said sweetly.

Taylor looked at her like she wanted to hit her. "You shouldn't have blown all your money on crack and heroin." She didn't say this in a jokey way. Everyone looked at each other in silence.

Taylor called over to the bar. "Gloria can I have my bill please?" Gloria shook her head smiling. "Dennis has paid for your table. You lot don't owe anything."

Leah and Natasha clinked their glasses and Dave smiled. Taylor didn't look grateful though, she looked miserable. There was no pleasing some people. Jamie was pretending to be happy but Leah could tell his nose was out of joint. He obviously didn't like being outdone by Dennis.

What was strange though was Jess. She was staring very intently at Taylor who wasn't even looking at her. Leah recognised that look. It was the way Leah herself sometimes looked at her mum.

Part 2

SORT IT OUT: JAMIE
'Tell Me What All Your Fuss Is About, And I Will Try And Sort It Out Somehow.'

Chapter 7

TAYLOR'S FLIGHT SHOULD have landed two hours ago, she should be here any minute. Jamie hadn't seen her or Bennie for a week. The last time he saw her was the night before she flew back to the UK to visit her family when flash Dennis had paid for all their drinks. She'd seemed a bit distant that night, not really herself. Jamie had a horrible feeling she might stay in Britain. He couldn't bear the thought of not seeing her or Bennie again.

He was finding it a struggle to join in the conversation even though it was only him, Natasha, Leah and Jess in the bar, apart from Gloria who was behind the bar of course. He couldn't really concentrate. Just then the door finally opened, an old man in a golfing top and a glamorous looking slightly tarty younger woman walked in and sat at the bar. It was no good. He couldn't even check if their flight had landed safely as he couldn't get internet on his phone. What if something had happened? It wasn't like her to be late.

"Gloria have you changed the Wi-Fi password?" he called out, more in hope than anything else.

"Nope. Still gloria´s 123 small letters." said Gloria as she served the couple who had just walked in.

"Well it's not working." he grumbled, to no one in particular.

Natasha looked at her phone. "Mine's working but mine ain't from 1992 or whenever that piece of shit's from Jamie."

"Sorry I'm not a pop star and I can't afford the latest phone." muttered Jamie not bothering to look up.

"I ain't a pop star no more. I've got no money. But even I wouldn't be seen dead with that phone." she said it as a joke of course, not in a nasty way, Natasha didn't have a nasty side, she was only having banter, but Jamie hadn't thought about her being broke before.

He knew of course that she'd blown her money on drugs, everyone knew that, but he hadn't ever thought about the implications of that before now. He didn't like the thought of her struggling. Maybe he could help her out, they were hiring at his work after all. "I can get you a job if you want Tasha."

"Doin' what?"

"Doing what I do, surveying people over the phone."

Leah looked at him like he was mad. "That sounds like hell!" she said in disgust, staring at him like he'd just thrown a poo at her.

"Actually it's not as bad as you'd think. It's..." Words failed him. He couldn't lie. If he was going to get Natasha a job there he'd better be honest with her. "yeah it's hell but you get good money. Actually that's not true but you get some money." He said this to Natasha even though it was Leah who he was answering.

Leah and Natasha were a bit of a double act. They seemed to have the closest individual friendship of anyone in the group and Leah was quite protective of her. Although Leah would pick on everyone in their group, Jess in particular but Jamie himself included, she never picked on Natasha. It was odd when you thought about it considering she had the most ammunition on Natasha, everyone knew about her drug addiction and her songs and TV show. There was a lot of material there if you enjoyed picking on people as Leah clearly did. She would make lighthearted jokes about her music, but that was it. Maybe she was embarrassed though, Action Five-Sixteen had murdered Natasha's ex boyfriend after all.

Jess looked at Leah and said, "You haven't worked since you've been here Leah. How do you survive?"

"By minding my own business."

"Fine. I was only asking. I love being a music teacher. Not just because the money's good but because you get to help children develop their creativity. That's important and they don't focus much on that side of education in the UK."

"Yeah, you're so right Jess. They're always wasting time on English literature and biology and mathematics when they could be singing Kumbaya and banging a tambourine. Stupid British education system."

Jamie decided to stop this argument by changing the subject. Although actually it was them who'd changed the subject, so it would be more accurate to say he decided to go back to the original subject. "Tasha? Want me to sort it?"

"Nah I don't think I'd like it."

"No you wouldn't. No one there likes it, but it pays the rent."

She smiled at him but shook her head. "Nah you're alright. Thanks though."

Leah sat up and looked at them all like she was about to propose a toast. "Anyway, as I was saying, there's no such thing as bisexuals, just normal people and gays!"

Predictably, Jess didn't agree. "I'm going to ignore the '*normal people*' bit, and what you're saying is still stupid. What would you call someone who has relationships with both sexes Leah?"

"Oh, that's a gay! I'd call them a gay!"

"But they're not always gay. As I just said they have relationships with *both* sexes."

"They're gay. Once you've been a gay once you're a gay. Unless you don't do it again in which case you're an ex gay. But if you keep doing it, yeah, you're gay."

"No Leah. You're bisexual."

"No I'm not!"

"No thicko, I know *you're* not! I mean that's what someone who has relationships with men *and* women is called."

Natasha wouldn't usually get involved in Leah and Jess's political debates but she seemed to be following this one closely and even had an opinion of her own to add. "I'd guess either Sebastian or Poppy."

Jess looked completely lost. "What?"

Natasha elaborated. "A lot of people who fuck blokes and birds are called Sebastian or Poppy. Trust me. They're well bisexual names man. I've met loads called them names."

Jamie had never seen either Jess or Leah lost for words before but Natasha had completely stumped them both. This was brilliant! He decided to join in. "She's actually got a point! I work with a guy called Seb who's gay."

Jess looked at him in total seriousness then said, "I think that's probably a coincidence."

Natasha shook her head like a wise old professor. "No I don't think so man."

Jamie managed to keep a straight face as he said, "Yeah, I'm with Natasha on this one."

Poor Jess looked absolutely flabbergasted. "That's ridiculous. For one thing, I've got a friend called Poppy and she's.... Actually, Natasha might have a point here!"

Natasha smiled triumphantly. "Told ya. Bisexual names man."

Leah wasn't prepared to let this one go. "What would you call a man who has sex with ninety-nine women and one child? You'd call him a pedophile, wouldn't you? You wouldn't say 'oh he shags grown-ups and kids so he's by-pe-do!' One kid makes you a nonce, one gay makes you a gay. Simple."

Natasha laughed. "Taylor would love this convo man! What you just said Leah that sounds like a Taylor rant that does!"

It was true. Natasha was right, Taylor sometimes went on hilarious rants. It was great to see her do it. She could put a hilarious spin on anything. Sometimes she'd say quite shocking things, she was a bit like a risqué comedian doing a stand up routine. When she lost herself in a rant, this passion seemed to overtake her. Her face would light up and everyone would listen to her. It was like for a few minutes she became 'Taylor' rather than just 'Bennie's mum'. She was a fantastic mum of course, and Jamie loved how she was with Bennie but it was nice to see her get to be herself and be carefree, even if only for a two minute rant. And when she was in full swing her beauty seemed to somehow project itself and the whole bar was lit up.

She was really late now though. He looked at his phone again, just in case, but still no internet, he'd better tell the others. Maybe one of them could check her flight had landed or message her.

"She's back tonight. Her plane should have landed two hours ago, she should be here by now. I was trying to make sure she landed OK but can't get Wi-Fi so can't track her flight."

They didn't seem concerned. Instead Jess returned to the earlier subject. "Speaking of jobs, she has quite an interesting one, selling beauty products online. That must be fun to be your own boss."

Leah took this as a cue to attack. "Looking at the state of you I'm assuming you're not a regular customer?"

"No I'm not. A lot of those products are tested on animals."

"Oh, here we go again with the lecture! Jamie are your surveys tested on animals?"

"Not as far as I know Leah. Although being animals would be a step up for some of the people I speak to on a daily basis. And yeah you're right Jess, Taylor's job is pretty cool."

Leah looked at him like he'd missed something. "She seems to fly back and forth to England a lot which is a bit suspicious considering her dad is a major drug smuggler." she said.

"She goes there to visit her family."

"What family? Her dad lives in Northern Cyprus. He had to fuck off there when he was going to get extradited back to Britain. It's on his Wikipedia page. Google *Terry 'Stone Cold' Seavers armed robber*."

"I can't, can I? I've got no Wi-Fi!" He wouldn't have googled it even if he did of course, he would have gone on the airline website.

"You know when she was three months old rival dealers burst into her house demanding money and held a shotgun to her face while she was in her mother's arms. They fired it and it was a blank cartridge but the noise left her deaf. She cured her deafness herself." said Jess. This was true, but not really relevant.

"If she'd known she was going to have to listen to your shit she probably wouldn't have bothered!" said Leah, but now Jamie was thinking. Surely Leah was on a wind up, did she really believe Taylor was smuggling drugs?

"Jokes aside, Leah do you really think she's smuggling drugs?" he asked.

"No." said Leah sarcastically. "I'm sure her dad left Dave in charge of the family business. Why wouldn't he?"

Natasha giggled and said, "It's so cringe when he claims he's a gangster. I do like him though, he is pretty funny."

"He's a harmless guy and he's very sweet, he's just confused." said Jess.

"So it's pretty unlikely he'd be left in charge of an international drugs cartel. Taylor on the other hand... Well, she really is stone cold." said Leah smiling.

"True she is as cold as a snowman's pocket and she's proper smart and clued up." Natasha remarked.

"Yeah. You can tell if the law turned up she wouldn't crumble under pressure. Dave would probably start rapping at them."

As Leah said this Natasha burst out laughing.

Jess came back to Taylor's defence, "Who says there's even still a drugs cartel to run? As I understand it, her father made his money out of armed robberies and was one of the first armed robbers to invest his money into drugs. Then he fled to Spain and then as you say to Northern Cyprus. He might have made his money and gone legal now."

Leah sneered at her. "Yeah, he's probably got a paper round hey Jess?"

Jamie felt he'd better help Jess out here. "And he wasn't even with Taylor's mum at the time. He moved out here with Dave cause Dave and Taylor have got different mums, Taylor grew up in Rochdale with her mum. Then he fucked off and left Dave here. As far as I'm aware he hasn't given either of them any of his money, he obviously doesn't give a fuck about them. You don't know what you're talking about Leah."

He'd never lost his temper with any of them before. He'd said his piece now and decided it would be best not to join in this conversation anymore. Anyway Jess seemed happy to take over the role of defending Taylor.

"And she always brings Bennie back to England with her. She wouldn't put him in danger like that." said Jess.

"If I was smuggling gear I'd bring a kid. Look the innocent single mum. Come on! Are you lot stupid? She's the coldest criminal I've met."

"Well that's impressive considering the scum and murderers you were friends with in England Leah."

Natasha put her head in her hands looking frustrated and annoyed. "Oh Jess for fucks sake man! One night without the politics shit man, please."

It was odd that she'd pick on Jess for slagging off Action Five-Sixteen killers. Then Jess sort of took the words out of Jamie's mouth, well not mouth cause he wasn't going to say it, but brain. She took the words out of his brain.

"Natasha how can you be friends with Leah? Action Five-Sixteen killed your boyfriend!"

As she said this, at the exact same moment as each other Leah yelled "Shut up Jess!" And Natasha yelled "Ex boyfriend!" And they both glared at Jess with venom.

Jess looked taken aback by this. "I see. I wish they'd kill mine! That's a joke of course. But it must be weird to hang out with an ex A-Five-Sixteen member."

She said this in a much gentler way than she'd said it before. Her whole tone had changed.

"It weren't Leah though was it?" said Natasha. In a way which Jamie felt sounded like she wasn't sure.

"Exactly!" said Leah smirking. Then, doing a sarcastic impression of Jess she continued, "You can't tar a whole group of people just because of the actions of a few idiots!"

To be fair it was quite a good impression. They all laughed, even Jess, who still laughing, said, "Well done Leah. You've actually beaten me in an argument."

Leah looked absolutely delighted with herself. "Yay! Gloria! Can I have a bottle of that white wine muck that you call champagne please? The one that costs three euros in the supermarket and you sell for ten euros. You know? The one creepy men on golfing holidays buy for prostitutes to look flash! I'm celebrating!"

At this point the old man in the golfing top and the glamorous looking young tarty woman who were together at the bar put down their 'champagne' and stormed out.

Natasha howled with laughter.

"Oh Leah!" moaned Gloria, looking annoyed.

"Oops!" said Leah. She didn't seem sorry at all. Jamie was just wondering whether she'd done it on purpose or not when Taylor entered the bar pushing Bennie in a buggy. He was clutching a new looking teddy bear.

Jamie jumped up to greet her. "There you are! We were getting worried. Were you delayed?"

"No. I had to buy someone a new bear, didn't I Bennie?"

"Mummy had to do operation to get medicine out of him." said Bennie.

"Did he die?" asked Leah.

"No he not die, stupid idiot head!" yelled Bennie, looking really angry.

Taylor rubbed his head. "Hey calm down captain grumpy."

Gloria yelled out from behind the bar, "Guess what I've got over here Bennie? Oreo-cake and a balloon!"

Bennie ran behind the bar clutching his bear and Gloria handed him the cake and balloon. He ate the cake, got back in his buggy holding the balloon and promptly fell asleep. Taylor wiped the mess of cake from round his mouth but he didn't wake.

"His teddy seems to get ill and you have to take the medicine out quite a lot." said Leah. Now Jamie thought about it that was true.

"Yeah, it's pretty much every flight." said Taylor distractedly, as she licked a tissue and wiped the corner of Bennie's mouth.

Leah smiled at Jamie, and he tried not to look at her. He decided to change the subject. Fast.

"So how was sunny England?"

Taylor turned round and looked at him."What? Have you forgotten what it's like there already?" she asked.

Jamie realised that when he was with Taylor, when he looked into her eyes, when he lost himself in her hypnotic beauty then yes, he had forgotten.

Chapter 8

EIGHT MONTHS AGO, EXMOUTH, Devon

Jamie had always got on better with girls than with boys. He wasn't a sissy, he was just, he felt, an individual. Girls were allowed, even encouraged, to be unique but boys had to fit into a category. You were a casual or a goth or a skater or whatever. And boys tended to group together based on which genre they fitted into. Jamie never felt he fitted into any of these groups so he didn't have such close friendships with boys. He liked football and beer for example, but he had no desire or inclination to go and watch Exeter play, or wear designer clothes, or get involved in this Action Five-Sixteen thing that they were all into now. (Some of the lads he'd been at school with had just been arrested for a violent protest where they'd tried to disrupt a local Eid celebration event.) And he liked playing the guitar but not leather jackets or long hair. And he even had a skateboard but he wasn't obsessed with it and he only rode it occasionally, in the summer, and he quite liked alternative music but he didn't think anyone who didn't was a prick. And... so that was why he got on better with girls.

Carly who was the same age as him had been his best friend on and off since they were four years old. Their mums had been friends since they were teenagers. She looked older than him now though, Jamie realised that's what a couple of years of heroin addiction will do. You could see she'd once been beautiful and the damage wasn't irreparable but she needed to sort herself out fast and Jamie knew that as her friend, he needed to help her. He felt like they'd had a breakthrough tonight but he'd thought that before and been wrong.

They were sitting on the couch in Jamie's living room although it was a studio flat so technically they were sitting in every room. His flat was small and a mess but he liked it. There was a guitar leaning against the wall and posters of bands including The Rat Pack, and classic films such as *Casablanca*, *The Godfather*, *Reservoir Dogs*, *Fight Club*, *Snatch* and *The Italian Job* on the walls.

"We've been here before Carly."

Carly said nothing and just stared into space, aimlessly flicking cigarette ash into a beer can which was already overflowing with cigarette butts.

Jamie stared at her. "Carly?!"

"I know Jago. I know. But what can I do?"

"You can leave him! For fucks sake!"

"Easy for you to say"

"It is easy. Look at me. I'm not going out with him. Try doing that."

Carly snorted a laugh, "Yeah, I know what you're saying Jago. I know what you're saying. And I know you're right. But you know me better than anyone, how long we been friends?"

"Obviously, a long time cause you tagged me in a photo of us when we were about seven standing by a paddling pool in your mum's garden. I was wearing shorts and a WWF T-shirt and I'm holding a plastic sword and trying to look hard. Thanks for uploading that by the way. I'm so glad the world got to see it!"

"Sorry Jago. I'm sorry, I just liked it cause it reminded me of a happier time."

"You remember when the photo was taken?"

"No. But it was a long time ago, so it was a happier time."

"Jesus. I can probably speak to your mum you know? Maybe you could move back in with her." Jamie still saw Carly's mum sometimes. He'd bumped into her the week before in fact in the Tesco express. She liked Jamie and always seemed pleased to see him, she might listen to him.

"She threw me out Jago. She threw me out. And she said she never wants to see me again. That was eleven years ago so I'd say she means it."

"She said she'll see you when you're clean! You stole your dead nan's jewellery out of your mum's room and sold it for heroin. Surely you can see why she was pissed off?"

"Why bring it up Jago? Why?"

"Sorry but I'm just saying I could talk to her."

"But I'm not clean am I? I'm still using. So she won't want to see me will she?"

"I still don't see why you won't move in here with me."

"Because either Kevin would steam through the door and stab you, and me probably or I'd start clucking and that Gibson lesbian guitar would be straight down the pawnbrokers and I'd lose you then. I'm not up for that."

"It's actually a Gibson Les Paul guitar but yeah, I'd be pissed off if you sold it for brown."

"Exactly. So here we are."

"Ok silly idea I'm sure but, why not get clean?"

"It costs ten grand for effective rehab and twenty quid for a bag that'll sort me. I've got twenty quid."

Jamie had ten thousand seven hundred pound in his bank. It had taken him ages to save and was earmarked for a deposit on a flat. With his job a mortgage should be no problem but he'd need a substantial deposit as he was on his own. Saving the money had been much harder than earning it. You didn't miss anything when you were at work, except maybe Jeremy Kyle, and he wasn't that fussed on that, but when you were saving you missed out on things. No takeaways, no holidays, he'd been rationing his cigarettes to five per day, only buying supermarket own brand booze and he didn't have a car. Then there were the countless nights out he'd missed, even the Missing Andy gig which he wanted to go to and was only a tenner for a ticket, but he'd have had to have bought drinks there and got a cab and in the end he couldn't justify the expense. He looked at Carly and imagined it was him, withered by drug abuse, about to spend twenty pound on heroin, desperate not to but feeling trapped, with no way out. He knew what the right thing to do was, but even if he looked at this from a purely selfish point of view, which would make him happier this time next year, his own flat or Carly getting her life back?

"Yeah? I've got ten grand."

Carly burst into tears. "Jago, no!!"

"I'm doing this. You'd do it if it was the other way round."

Carly said nothing but nodded her head manically whilst still crying.

"One thing though, when you're clean and don't look like an old bag anymore I'm getting a shag off you!"

Carly laughed hysterically. "Jago! I can't believe you just said that! That is so not you!"

"Yeah well. Your boyfriend's already beaten me up hasn't he so what can he do?"

" You know I'm so sorry about that, Kevin just gets a bit... Kevin's a cunt."

"Well said! On that note, I'm going to bed. Night Carly, dream about what you'll do when you're clean yeah?"

Jamie put up the fold up bed and got in it while Carly curled up on the sofa, smiling.

Jamie looked up at the ceiling and smiled to himself. He felt good. She was definitely going to get clean and free of that prick this time, her and her mum could sort things out then. Jamie could arrange that easily when Carly was clean. There were worse things you could spend ten grand on.

Chapter 9

JAMIE WAS IN A WINE bar with his manager Geoff after work. He didn't really like wine bars, he much preferred pubs but Geoff had asked him to come for a drink after work. Even in his suit which Jamie had to wear for work he still felt very out of place. There was a big tennis match on the TV so the bar was packed and they were standing by the door constantly having to move out of people's way which made it hard to talk. They were both drinking bottles of Peroni, which was the only beer they served in there. He was gasping for a cigarette but Geoff didn't smoke and the fact they didn't have a table meant Jamie would have to leave Geoff standing by the door on his own if he went out for one. He thought that might appear rude so he didn't do it. He'd have to wait and have one later.

Geoff explained that the company was expanding and he wanted to make Jamie a team leader from next month. It would mean more money and he felt Jamie would be perfect for the role. He was to attend a meeting in Geoff's office where they would discuss it properly next Monday.

Jamie was delighted. The extra money would come in handy, especially now that he'd given Carly all his savings. And it felt good getting recognition for his work. Jamie knew that he'd been doing well there recently, he'd finished top of the board out of twenty-four salespeople the last two months in a row. Geoff had a theory about why this was.

"You're not like most salesmen. You actually care about people. And in the life insurance game that helps. That's why you sell as much as you do. Because when people purchase a life insurance policy they do it because they care. They care about those they leave behind. And you care about people Jamie. That's why you're such an asset to this business."

Jamie was grateful for the compliment and he thanked Geoff but he felt it would be wrong for him to take all the credit. He was sure the leads had improved dramatically in the last two months. He asked Geoff if it was different data and Geoff smiled and admitted that it was. The company had always bought their leads from offshore call centres, Geoff explained, usually based in India or the Philippines and the staff there had strong foreign accents. As a consequence the UK consumers could not resist winding them up so would tell them a load of nonsense, which meant a lot of the leads were rubbish. Jamie knew this was true. Some of the names for example that they got were ridiculous. Jamie had personally had a 'Mac-Donald Zmeal', a 'Sir Dan Hussein', a 'Barry Yakaboma', he'd once got all the way to arranging a quote for a 'Scott Jegg' before he twigged.

Geoff explained that for the past two months they'd been buying their data from a call centre in Fuengirola, Spain. This call centre only hired English expats so the quality of information was much better. Jamie was just telling Geoff that his cousin Gloria owned a small bar there when a posh looking woman walked towards the door to go out for a cigarette. Jamie moved out the way and that was when he saw her across the road out the corner of his eye. He looked again. It was her. He felt sick. "Will you excuse me a moment?" He asked Geoff, and handed him his near empty bottle without waiting for a reply, he walked out and crossed the road.

Her and Kevin were sitting on the pavement. It wasn't cold but her lips had that slightly blue look and there were red patches round her eyes.

"Carly! What the fuck! You're off your nut aren't you?"

Carly looked like she was just waking up. "I'm sorry Jago. I'm sorry." Her voice slurred as she spoke. She sounded like she was about to fall asleep.

"You had a chance to sort it out! I gave you a chance! I gave you everything I had!"

"Life is what it is Jago. Life is what it is."

"I really can't believe this."

"What do you want me to say? I'm sorry. I'll pay you back all of it one day."

"I can't believe you'd rather do smack with this loser than sort yourself out."

Kevin who looked so out of it that he might as well have had a needle sticking out of his arm, looked Jamie up and down like he was a piece of shit, even though Jamie was wearing a suit and Kevin was wearing track suit bottoms and a baseball cap and sitting on the pavement.

"Who you calling a loser cunt? Fuck off before I bang your face open again. Prick."

Carly put her hand on Kevin's shoulder as if to restrain him, although despite his threat Kevin had made no effort to get up. Then she said, "I don't want trouble Jago. Just go. Please just go."

What else could he do? As he turned around Kevin yelled out. "Cheers for the money by the way. Mug."

Jamie ignored this and stormed back across the road, almost being hit by a car in the process which was forced to slam on its breaks. The driver hooted and shouted that Jamie was a 'fucking retard!' Very few people agree with an assessment of themselves delivered by an angry stranger from a moving car but Jamie agreed with that. He felt like a fucking retard. He went back into the bar and politely declined the team leader role. He asked if they were hiring at this call centre in Fuengirola, Geoff said he'd find out.

Two weeks later he was boarding the flight to Malaga on a one way ticket with a job to start the next week. It was time to move on. He never spoke to Carly again.

Chapter 10

JAMIE LOOKED AT TAYLOR, she was stroking Bennie's hair while he slept. How could she risk everything by smuggling drugs? Maybe someone like Leah would do it but Taylor? She was a mum. How would she feel if she was caught and her and Bennie were separated? Maybe for years? He was going to have to try and stop her doing this before it was too late. What was so gutting was that before today there was nothing, NOTHING that he didn't like about her.

In answer to her question, he now remembered exactly what England was like.

"No. I remember it. It's full of let downs and disappointment. Has been since I was at school." he said.

"You lot are so lucky going school man. I wish I'd went there." said Natasha cheerfully.

"You didn't go to school?" asked Taylor, looking shocked.

"Nah course not man I was in *Why Always Me?* from when I was six weren't I?"

Jamie pointed out that he still couldn't believe that was her. His little brother had loved that show. Jamie had occasionally watched it with him. It was weird to think he was mates with the star.

"So you never had to go school?" asked Taylor.

"Nah we had a tutor in a caravan on the set. There was only like, five of us in the class."

"What was that like?" asked Jess.

"It was a doss! People think kids are stupid but we knew we could get her fired anytime but they couldn't replace us. We just used to fuck about in there. But I don't think she cared cause she got to meet all the celebs that came on the show. We had loads man, Posh Spice, Craig from Big Brother, Dane Bowers, Lisa Kudrow, James Corden. But he weren't that famous then."

"Being in the limelight from the age of six must have been tough." said Jess. Jamie had never thought of that before.

Before Natasha could answer Leah interrupted, "Bet the money helped though. What did you spend it all on by the way?"

Natasha laughed, she laughed at most things Leah said. "Fuck's sake Leah man, you know what I spent it on!"

Leah winked at Jamie. "Oh yeah. I don't blame you though Natasha. It's the evil smugglers I blame!"

This made Jamie feel very uncomfortable so he would normally have been grateful for a distraction. However the distraction that came was Dennis coming into the bar. On reflection Jamie would have taken feeling a bit uncomfortable over having to see him.

"Hi guys. I'm not being rude but I am bursting for a piss. I'll be back in one sec." said Dennis as he ran past their table and into the gents toilet.

"Don't hurry back on our account. Make it a poo if you want." said Taylor, sharply.

That night when he was in bed unable to sleep and feeling terrible, Jamie reflected back on this and thought it was odd. Dennis popped into the bar a lot but somehow never when Taylor wasn't there. Today his timing couldn't have been better, and Jamie strongly suspected it wasn't a coincidence. He was sure Dennis had been waiting outside watching the bar for a while.

"Right, I'm off. It's been a long day." said Taylor as she hurriedly grabbed her things and wheeled Bennie (who was still fast asleep in his buggy) towards the door.

"Yeah I've got work tomorrow. I'll walk with you Taylor. See you lot later." said Jamie. He downed his drink and left the bar. He almost had to jog to catch up with her.

Chapter 11

LEAH KNEW TAYLOR WAS smuggling drugs. She'd worked it out ages ago, it was obvious. Even morons like Jamie and Jess should have clocked it. Every time she flew back from Britain she opened Bennie's teddy bear and did an operation to get 'medicine' out. Then she bought him a new bear. Leah didn't really have a problem with it, she had been joking about her outrage of 'evil smugglers'. That was just to wind Jamie up, in truth she thought it was genius. Customs would never take a teddy bear off a toddler who was clutching it tightly. She could breeze through. And she obviously had the connections to supply her in England and buy from her in Spain through her dad's network. Leah was impressed. What bothered her was Jamie and Jess acting like she was this angel who was so innocent when they were always so happy to think of Leah as scum. That got on her nerves.

Dennis came out the toilet and looked disappointed and a bit surprised. "Where are them two?" he asked.

Leah was just thinking that he couldn't count as there was actually three people missing and wondering which two he meant when Jess said, "They left. Think she was tired. They've had a long day, what with the flight and stuff."

Dennis nodded but said nothing. Leah felt a tiny bit awkward so she asked a question. "Dennis, how did you get that scar?"

"Well Leah, between us lot I'm sure you know Tay's family have a rival family."

"The ones who made her deaf with the shotgun?" asked Jess.

"Yeah, well they found me once and wanted to know where Tay and Bennie was. Think they was gonna threaten them or worse to get to her dad you know? Anyway, I wouldn't give them the info they wanted so they did this. Nice people! But Tay and Bennie were safe and that's the main thing right? You won't say I told you lot this will you? She's a very private lady as you know. Anyway, you can't get involved with one of that family and not end up with a scar. I would have stood out in family photos at weddings and christenings and stuff wouldn't I?"

Leah laughed, and decided to ask another question. "Dennis while we're telling secrets, why does Taylor always cut Bennie's teddy bears open and take medicine out?"

Dennis looked panicked and frightened. "You know about that?"

"Yeah. Is she smuggling drugs?"

"Leah!" yelled Jess kicking her under the table.

"It's ok Jess. Look Taylor just does what she has to do to support her child. She's a single mum and it's tough mate. Thing is she comes from a family that makes money a certain way and... Well I just don't think she understands the risks. I'm making decent dough doing property investments out here and I just wanna look after them both you know? Hopefully soon she won't have to do it anymore. I just hope it won't be too late. As I said don't repeat this. I'm sure she'd have told you yourself. If she was closer to you lot."

Leah smirked at Jess but Jess wouldn't look at her. That cleared a lot up. Taylor obviously didn't trust them. Leah didn't really blame her though. She wouldn't tell people if she smuggled drugs. But Dennis had raised a good point, no matter what Jess and Jamie thought, Taylor obviously didn't feel close to them.

Chapter 12

AS THEY GOT ABOUT THREE minutes down the road, Jamie decided to say something. He knew he had to and he'd just been working out how to phrase it best. Bennie was still asleep and Taylor was pushing the buggy with him in.

"I can get you a job Taylor."

Taylor smiled at him but looked a bit confused. "Thanks Jamie but I've got a job. I need to work from home to look after him."

She obviously hadn't thought this through properly, what the possible consequences could be. She was being naive.

"Taylor what you're doing is stupid. What if you got caught? What would happen to him?"

"Caught selling make up?"

"Opening his bear? Taking 'medicine' out? You're so much better than that Taylor."

Jamie had never seen Taylor's face show a great deal of emotion before but he saw a lot now. She looked deeply hurt and disappointed

"Is that what you think of me? You think I'm a drug smuggler?" She almost whispered this as if she'd lost her voice and she looked shocked and heartbroken. It was like she was trying not to cry.

"I'm not judging you I'm trying to help."

"Well I'm judging you as a horrible friend. That's how low you think of me? Do you know that years before he was born when I was seventeen I took an overdose and had to be rushed to hospital and have my stomach pumped? And do you know that a nasty, spiteful, horrible person told him about that? And he had nightmares for months? Do you realise that every time he gets nervous he thinks his teddy needs its stomach pumped or it will die? Do you know he gets nervous when he flies? You think I'm the kind of mother who stuffs her kid's toys with cocaine? Thanks Jamie. Thanks for your opinion of me. Fuck you."

He called out after her as she walked off but she ignored him. He'd been wrong about people before of course but he knew, one hundred percent that she was telling the truth. And he felt sick.

Part 3

BREATHLESS: NATASHA

'I Don't Wanna Be, I Don't Ever Wanna Be Like Everybody else. I Don't Wanna be, I Don't Really Wanna Be Like Anybody Else.'

Chapter 13

NATASHA LOVED HANGING out in Gloria's bar, especially when they were all together as a group like today. She missed Sophie of course. Sophie was her sister, she was three years older than Natasha and she ran her own business, a nail salon, she'd been running it for a year so she'd been in charge of a business since she was twenty-two! How cool was that? Sophie and Natasha looked alike, they'd both inherited their grandad Trev's Jamaican features but had green eyes and blonde curly hair (although Sophie straightened hers). Natasha always felt Sophie looked more intelligent than her, which she was obviously, she was a business woman. Natasha loved it when people said they looked alike though, that was her favorite compliment.

Even though she missed Sophie she felt lucky to have such good mates. There was Leah of course, Leah reminded her of Sophie in a way, she was tough and she seemed to understand how things worked, she was like a big sister to Natasha. Then there was Jamie and Jess, they were both so sweet and kind and caring, Natasha felt they should be a couple, they'd be kind to each other and if they had a kid it would be a well lucky baby having them as parents. And Taylor, she was so funny she cracked Natasha up with her rants. Taylor was how she'd met the others, she'd just arrived in Spain and she'd stopped outside Gloria's to admire Bennie cause he was so adorable and she'd got talking to Taylor who'd told her how she'd only just moved there herself and invited her in for a drink, which was when she met Jamie and Jess. They'd both been in Spain about the same amount of time as each other which was just longer than Taylor, and then Leah arrived about three months after Natasha. She liked Dave as well. He was so funny especially when he rapped and although he always flirted with Natasha and he clearly fancied her, he wasn't creepy. She liked Dennis as well. He was always kind to her and he called her 'mate' no one had ever called her that before but she liked it, Dennis was friendly like that. He wasn't in Gloria's today though, all the others were there.

Natasha knew she wasn't as clever as the others in some ways. She didn't really have any political opinions and even if she did she'd never be able to express them how Leah and Jess could. And Jamie often talked about things she didn't understand, and Taylor used words in her rants sometimes which Natasha had no idea what they meant. In one way though she knew she was doing better than any of them. She was *coping* better than them. Basically she was better at being an expat.

People think when they move abroad that's all they've done but Natasha knew there was more to it than that. You didn't just move to another country, you became an expat, and that was a massive thing in itself, like becoming a vegan or a parent or a Hindu or something. Taylor once told her that when Bennie was born she became Bennie's mum, like she just got this whole new identity. Expats don't realise they get that too. Suddenly no friends, no family, no familiar surroundings, no history even. It can feel lonely, very lonely. Natasha was coping better than the others and she knew why. She'd effectively been an expat since she was six years old. One of her earliest memories of feeling sad was being in a really flash hotel one night cause she was filming on location and seeing a group of kids in the street messing around. She didn't know them, but she felt like she did. She felt like they were the kids she grew up with, because she knew that somewhere out there, the kids she grew up with were messing around and she was left out. Eventually the security from the hotel chased them and they ran off. She wished she could run with them.

She knew she was the happiest of the Gloria's bunch and the most cheerful. The others all gave off a slight vibe of sadness and depression. She'd never tell them that of course, she knew they couldn't help it, most expats gave off that vibe. Natasha had read the novel *Oliver Twist* by Charles Dickens, (OK she hadn't actually read the book. But she knew the story cause she'd seen the film *Oliver!* thousands of times. They'd watched it loads when she was little, cause Sophie had played Nancy in a drama production at the local theatre in Bolton. Sophie was a great Nancy, she did the London accent and everything and she sang beautifully) but the point was, Natasha understood why they ended it when they did, cause they wanted a happy ending. If they'd let it go on to its *real* conclusion she knew one hundred percent what would happen and very few other people did. She knew that Oliver would leg it from Mr. Brownlow or whatever he was called, and run back to Fagin's gang as fast as his little legs would carry him. If not back to Mr. Bumble and the orphanage to happily moan about the gruel ration. It didn't matter that he had a better life now. It wasn't *his* life. It wasn't where he belonged. Eventually everyone tries to find their way home. In some ways, *E.T.* was actually more realistic than *Oliver Twist*.

She'd recently read an article in a magazine about this lad who'd been in the paper and on TV cause he was a dust man who won the lottery and he'd blown all the money on drugs and parties and a massive racetrack and cars to race and now he was skint. The magazine was saying it like the bloke was an idiot but Natasha didn't think he was. If you asked the kids on the estate she grew up on in Bolton what they'd do if they got money you'd get answers like that, dirt tracks and race cars and things. If you asked in a posh area they'd say sensible things like 'bonds' and 'stocks' and 'property portfolio' words Natasha didn't understand. It was cause those kids *expected* to get big money at some point and the kids on the Bolton estate didn't. So for them it was a daydream with no basis in reality. But what if it became reality? Well then as Natasha and the lottery dustman well knew, you could be in trouble. She supposed it was different in the old days. You were either born lord or lady something in which case you'd be loaded. Or you weren't in which case you'd be like a servant or chambermaid or chimney-sweep or something and you'd always be skint. At least you were prepared.

"So, Friday. I say we start here then hit the strip. Let's get absolutely hammered!" said Leah.

Natasha hated the strip. She only really liked being in Gloria's.

"Oh not the strip man I hate it. Dickheads coming up asking me for photos and singing my songs at me every five minutes." she said.

"But we get put in the VIP section with you there! Unless there's, you know? More important famous people there, like the time that guy who plays for Leyton Orient was there, or when the Cheeky Girls walked in and we got moved." said Leah, both those things had previously happened.

Dave shook his head and said, "Nah, we was in VIP cause I was there. Trust me, I'm known innit? Man runs dat strip!" There was actually some truth in this. Dave did get special treatment in clubs, although it was on the understanding that he 'say hi to your old man from me yeah? Tell him we looked after you.' So it wasn't really Dave's achievement as such.

Taylor frowned. "Well I can't go. Don't think they let three year olds in. Which is outrageous when you think about it. People getting balloons, kicking off, rolling round on the floor, then being sick? That's what he does every day!"

Jamie laughed, "True! I was going to say actually Taylor, I've got him a ticket to the Malaga game on Friday. You go with these guys."

Natasha noticed that was the first thing either Jamie or Taylor had actually said to each other all day, which was unusual.

"Really? That's incredible! He'd love to go to a real football match. You don't mind taking him?" asked Taylor.

"I'd love to take him! Have a boy's night out. It will be fun. You enjoy yourself. Me and Bennie will have a right laugh."

"How much was the ticket?"

"Don't be silly! Child's ticket costs next to nothing. I'll take him for a burger after then he can come round mine. You can pick him up later."

"Thanks Jamie. I won't stay out long. Probably about midnight?"

"Cool. He's welcome to crash at mine if you do wanna stay out late."

Taylor thanked him then got up and went to the toilet.

Bollocks. She was going to have to go to the strip. She really didn't want to but if even Taylor did then she was well outvoted.

"That is so lovely of you to take him to football." said Jess looking at Jamie.

"He's a great kid and we'll have fun. Anyway, she needs a night out. She hasn't been herself at all lately."

Jess looked impressed. "You're so perceptive Jamie. I've noticed that too. She seems to have lost her spark a little. I think it's since Dennis turned up."

"Yeah, I think so too." said Jamie. And he sounded a bit angry as he said it. Natasha had no idea what they were on about.

"Oh. You don't like Dennis, Jamie? Well that's shocking news! Why not?" said Leah. What was confusing was that Natasha felt it *was* shocking that Jamie didn't like Dennis but she thought Leah was being sarcastic.

"I don't dislike him as such, it's more, well, he reminds me of my stepdad."

"The one whose grave you said you'd piss on?" asked Jess, nodding enthusiastically as if to say she agreed.

Jamie nodded but still looked annoyed. Sometimes it really felt like Natasha was watching a series and had missed an episode.

"I bet you'd hate *all* of Taylor's ex boyfriends. In fact I think they'd all remind you of stepdads you hate!" said Leah

"Whatever. I'll be back in a sec, get us another pint Jess if you're ordering." mumbled Jamie as he got up and went to the toilet.

Chapter 14

JAMIE HAD MESSAGED her of course. He'd sent a really long message explaining and trying to apologise and she'd said it was all OK but he wanted to say it to her face, he owed her that. Finally she came out the toilet.

"You waiting for the ladies toilet Jamie? Have you had some life changing operation we should know about?"

"I just wanted to apologise about the other night, I don't think you're a drug smuggler."

She looked at him like he'd missed the point. "No but you *did*. I don't give a shit what people think of me but for you of all people to think that, to think that that's the kind of mum I am, that really, really hurt Jamie."

She didn't point out that she shouldn't have to explain private things about her past in order to clear herself of false accusations, that as a loyal friend she should be able to rely on his trust unconditionally. But the implication was, he felt quite clear from the look on her face and the tone of her voice. And she'd be right of course. He felt like shit.

"Taylor I just didn't think it through. You're my friend and I worship the ground you walk on. If I think you or Bennie are in trouble then I panic and try and help. I should have thought about it before I accused you and I'd have realised how silly it was. I'm so sorry. Can I buy you a sorry drink?"

She smiled. "Well. You are taking my son to football so... Yeah you can buy me a couple of drinks and I'll forget it."

'You of all people' she said. *'I wouldn't want you of all people to think that.'* What did she mean him of all people? He knew it, he knew there was something here. He was buzzing.

Chapter 15

NATASHA FELT EYES ON her. You know when you're being stared at before you even look but you also know *how* you're being stared at. You feel good and then see a fit bloke checking you out for example, well Natasha felt threatened. Then she saw him.

There was a creepy guy who'd just walked into the bar staring at her. People often stared at her of course, and she'd learned to live with it. 'The price of fame' people called it but Natasha disagreed with that, she felt she'd paid the price of fame several times over, this was more like the hidden charges of interest added to the price. Most people were harmless enough and just sang her songs at her or took photos. But creepy people scared her. She'd received some quite frightening messages before and some of the creepy men had been horrible, like the guy who kept offering her money for her used socks, or the guy who said he'd kill his dog if she didn't sleep with him. This guy looked that type. He was about fifty odd and looked really slimy.

Jamie and Taylor had just rejoined the table, Natasha wouldn't have noticed that until Leah said, "Jamie did you just follow her to the toilet?!"

Dave looked at Jamie like he was delighted that he'd just seen him fall into a trap."Errr! You dirty boy!" He yelled, with all the enthusiasm of a playground bully.

Leah smirked, "You know that's not OK right?"

Jamie looked annoyed and said "Leah if you've got-" Before he could finish whatever he was going to say, the weird man interrupted him.

The weird man had walked over to their table like a zombie from *The Walking Dead* completely transfixed on Natasha, then said to her, "It's you. Isn't it?"

Taylor gave him a 'fuck off you weirdo' look and said, "You do realise that whoever you say that to, the answer will always be yes?"

The weird man still didn't take his eyes off Natasha. "Whatever. Can I take you out sometime Natasha?"

She smiled politely, "Nah you're alright."

He looked agitated and a bit aggressive. "Just come out for a drink with me, look, I realise I'm old enough to be your-"

"Attacker?" interrupted Taylor.

Finally the weird man looked away from her. He looked at Taylor. "What do you mean by that?"

Taylor stared back. She wasn't scared. "Listen, I understand that you've wanked over this moment a lot, and as you sat on your toilet exploding into your tissue it went really well in your head but no, just no. And not just with Natasha but any woman in the world."

"You don't even know me!" screamed the weird man.

Taylor nodded and said, "True. But it's impossible to imagine you having sex with anyone without picturing them screaming for help."

The weird man looked like he was going to say or do something horrible. He looked at them all in turn, each of them stared back at him. He thought better of it and sheepishly walked out the bar. Natasha could have hugged Taylor. What would she have done if she'd been on her own? She couldn't have handled it like Taylor did. She really loved this group.

"Taylor that was unbelievable!" said Jess

Leah rolled her eyes and said "Here comes the lecture..."

"Fuck off Leah. I meant how you handled that for Natasha that was brilliant." snapped Jess

Natasha thought it was brilliant too.

"I thought it was going be one of those 'in a democracy everyone has the right to say whatever' blah, blah, blah!" said Leah.

"Sorry Leah. I forgot how much you hate democracy." said Jess. Natasha wasn't sure exactly what 'democracy' meant, but she didn't think Jess was sorry.

"I do actually! Any system where the opinion of two idiots is worth more than the opinion of one genius is flawed." said Leah smiling.

"Oh look everyone! Skilton's a ventriloquist! Roll up and watch his puppet talk!" yelled Jess at them all. Sometimes Natasha felt they really might as well have been speaking Japanese.

Jess then looked at Taylor and rolled her eyes but then Taylor went on a rant.

"I'm sorry Jess but I agree with Leah on this, democracy's fucked up, think about it. Gang rape's a form of democracy. You've got ten people, nine want a rough shag and one's screaming for them to stop, oh well, majority rules, tough shit love. Fuck democracy."

"Where's Dennis, Taylor?" asked Jamie smiling

"Gone to the UK to visit his family, why?"

Jamie winked at Jess and she smiled back at him.

Natasha didn't always get the little subtle gestures, some of them went right over her head, but she got that one. What Jamie and Jess were saying, well not saying as such but what they meant was that Taylor was more herself and fun when Dennis wasn't around.

Then they all talked about the creepy man again.

Jess asked her if she was OK and Leah said she'd walk her home when they left just in case he was still there. Dave asked her if she wanted to borrow his machine gun which prompted a conversation about whether he had one or not. Jamie said Dave was talking rubbish and asked Dave if it was an invisible machine gun. Dave said if Jamie carried on he'd find out as Dave would shoot him in a drive by. Jamie pointed out that Dave didn't have a car, then asked if he had an invisible car to match his invisible machine gun. Taylor then looked a bit annoyed with Jamie. Jamie then told Taylor how she'd handled the creepy man brilliantly and how impressed he was.

"And that, is why I don't wanna go to the strip." said Natasha.

"It must be so weird being recognised by strangers." said Jess

"Do you get used to it Tasha?" asked Jamie.

"I suppose."

Then Taylor said, "You know when we leave he's gonna come back and sniff your chair."

Natasha was horrified. She hadn't thought of that.

"Taylor! Why would you say that?! That's vile!" said Jess, laughing.

"Well, he looked like a chair sniffer to me." said Taylor.

"He was a bit creepy." admitted Jamie.

Taylor looked at him like he'd underestimated the perversions of the weird man. "A bit? He looked like he wanted to murder Tasha and rape her. In that order." she said.

"Is that order worse?" asked Leah.

"Of course! Imagine how degrading that is." said Taylor like it was a silly question which Leah had asked.

Jamie turned to Natasha and asked, "Is this the worst conversation you've ever had?"

"No." said Natasha. It wasn't either.

Chapter 16

SIX MONTHS AGO, BOLTON

It was the day before Sophie's wedding and Natasha was sitting in a magazine office opposite a female journalist called Linda who was aged about forty but desperately trying to look younger with her pink hair and glasses. There were framed photographs of various celebrities on the wall including Natasha as a child, when she was about six or seven and smiling a cheesy grin. She had a strong desire to grab that photo and rescue it from this place. Natasha didn't want to be in this office, she wanted to be with Sophie. She stared at the photo of herself.

"Are you sure you're OK?" asked Linda in a way that sounded more nosey than caring.

Natasha, who was on the verge of tears nodded.

"Let's get started shall we? What we're doing at the moment is a piece called *'Ten years later.'* Where I'm interviewing people who I interviewed ten years ago and seeing what's changed for you and in what ways. You were my youngest interview Natasha as you were only nine last time we met, anyway just relax and let's whizz through. Do you remember our last interview together?"

"No."

"I do. You were such a happy young girl, let's see some of your answers back then, here's a great one! I asked what you were going to do when you turned eighteen and received all your money. Do you remember your answer?"

"No."

"I'll read it, this is brilliant! You said, *'I'm gonna buy loads of ice cream and loads of chicken nuggets and a massive bed what's so high you need a trampoline to get on it and I'm gonna get builders to take the stairs out my house and make a water slide instead, cause it'll be dead funny when my mum has to slide downstairs cause she hates swimming, but me and Sophie, that's my sister, we'll love it!'"* She paused then said "I take it of course that you didn't do any of those things?"

"Obviously not. I spent it on crack cocaine and heroin mainly, as you well know."

Linda looked a bit thrown by that. "Yes, um... forgotten where I was now... Ah! For things you hate, your answer was, *'This girl called fat Emma, her name's*

Emma but we call her Fat Emma cause she's a massive ugly fattie! She lives on my street and she ate my lunch once, I hate her, she's a fat ugly, minging, gherkin.' What would your answer be now, things you hate, ten years later?"

"Dunno, journalists probably."

"Ouch! We're not all bad! Let's talk about your relationship with Kane Thomas."

"Let's not."

"It's literally just a couple of questions. Our readers will want to know about this, and it's a chance for you to tell your side of it."

"I'm not in a relationship with Kane no more."

"How did the relationship end?"

"Just did."

"But you're a witness for him in his upcoming murder trial?"

"I'm not allowed to talk about that."

"He is innocent you say?"

"I just told ya, I'm not allowed to discuss the case." said Natasha through gritted teeth. She was going to lose her temper with this woman in a minute. She could feel the anger welling up inside her.

"Ok. Let's talk about how you met. You told a journalist, '*I met Kane when I came out of rehab. He pulled up in this flash motor and started chatting me up, he admitted he was a drug dealer straight away, just weed and that he said, not hard stuff. Anyway, he told me to come out with him that night, said if I saw how much money dealers make I'd never take drugs again! I thought that was a pretty funny thing to say to someone who'd just come out of rehab to be fair.*

I really liked him. He weren't like other lads, he never licked my arse for one thing, he told me he thought my show was dead annoying when he was younger and he hated it! And he said I'm a great singer but he hated my records cause it ain't his type of music, I weren't used to that. And whenever I was with him people left me alone, no idiots approaching me, they didn't even look at me. I know why now, but he was always a gentleman at first in front of me. I didn't realise people were so scared of him then.'"

"No I never."

Linda looked confused. "You never what?"

"I never told *a journalist* all that. I told a girl who told me she was an ex addict, who said her ex-boyfriend was a yardie, who promised that we were mates and I could trust her with anything, who took me for a drink to celebrate us both being clean for six months, who waited till I was pissed out my head then started asking me loads of stuff, who turned out to be a lying, evil, undercover fucking journalist who'd never been in rehab or anything. She made it all up to get me to trust her then published all that stuff. Can we end this now please? My sister's getting married tomorrow and I want to be with her now."

"No problem at all. I didn't mean to upset you and I'm sorry if I have. I just had so much fun interviewing you ten years ago and I thought it would be great to catch up. One last question before you go?"

"One more."

"What would you say to teenagers who are tempted to use drugs?"

What a stupid question. "Nothing."

Linda looked a bit shocked, "You wouldn't tell them not to?"

"Why would they listen to me? I never listened to no one. They'll do it if they're gonna do it won't they? What the fuck can I do about it? Oh just put down what you like. You people always do don't you?"

Then Natasha got up and walked out, Linda was hurriedly writing something down and smiling to herself, Natasha was glad she hadn't cried in front of that bitch.

Chapter 17

THREE HOURS LATER SHE was sitting with Sophie in their parents living room. Their mum and dad were out decorating the hall for tomorrow so it was just the two of them.

They were drinking wine on the couch and had music from the TV on quietly in the background. Sophie had put on a playlist of eighties and nineties classics. Natasha would have done the same thing if she had chosen the music even though neither of them liked it. They had never discussed why they always did this but Natasha would do it so there was no chance that any of *her* songs would come on and she was sure Sophie did it for the same reason.

It was a nice house in an expensive part of town, (two Bolton players lived on the same street) it was probably the only good thing Natasha had done with her money. Sophie didn't live there anymore of course, she lived in a flat with Rob but she was staying there tonight cause Rob was in the flat and they couldn't see each other before the wedding. Natasha didn't live there either. She had a flat in London but even though neither of them lived there, Sophie seemed to be comfortable and much more at home there than Natasha. She'd go and open the fridge for example and knew where everything was and it was like she was the hostess and Natasha was a guest. As the sadness filled her and tried to escape through her eyes she held it in, firmly. This was Sophie's night and she wouldn't ruin it by being sad. She forced it back down and it settled as a lump deep in her throat. As she controlled and kept it there Sophie was talking.

"Mum and Dad obviously, and Rob's mum and stepdad and Rob's dad and his dad's girlfriend, and Kelly and Mark, and you obviously. And Nan. That's it I think. Oh and me and Rob of course."

Sophie looked at Natasha who was staring into space, then continued. "And Nigel of course! Tasha?"

"Yeah."

"You ain't listening to a word I'm saying are ya?"

"Course I am!"

"Yeah? Who's Nigel?"

Shit. "Nigel?"

"I was telling you who's on the top table. I knew you weren't listening so I said Nigel. We don't know a Nigel. I was catching you out."

"I weren't not listening. I was just thinking."

"Were you thinking about the trial?"

"No I was thinking about the wedding Sophie."

"Are you nervous?"

"About the trial?"

"I fucking *knew* you were thinking about that!"

"I weren't Soph, honest. You just brought it up man."

"This is the one day that's supposed to be about me. Not you. Me. Just one day that you ain't the star of, you can't even let me have that can ya? It's bad enough everyone else will make it all about you as usual. But now you are too."

"I ain't! Why do you hate me so much Soph? What have I done? I ain't even your maid of honour. I'm just a bridesmaid and I've never moaned, not once."

"Like I'd choose you over Kelly! She's my best mate. She's always been there for me, to be honest I wish you weren't even coming."

Natasha had heard the word 'heartbroken' before of course, and had probably used the expression loads herself but in that moment she actually understood exactly what it meant. What Sophie just said had broken her heart.

"Really Soph? You really wish that?"

"Do you blame me? My hen we go to Ascot and there's a picture of you in *Heat* magazine off your nut drinking champagne, no mention of me, it was *my* hen."

"The headline was *'Back to rehab?'* Do you think I wanted that?"

"My sixteenth we went to Disneyland cause *you* were on tour in America. Not for me. 'Oh we can't put your photos of your school prom up there Sophie, that's where Tasha's awards go.' Everywhere I go it's 'oh it's Natasha's sister' when I started my nail salon me and Rob had nothing. He had to work double shifts cause I was doing nails for free just for exposure. We lived on beans and toast for three months. And now it's successful and we can finally afford this wedding and not once, *not once* Tasha have Mum or Dad said they're proud of me. Tomorrow I'm going to walk down the aisle and become Mrs. Sophie McManamon, just one day of not being called Natasha's sister. I am going to walk down that aisle in a white dress, for the only time in my life, and all eyes will be on YOU. How do you think I fucking feel?"

Natasha burst into tears. She stood up and yelled in Sophie's face while still crying.

"I didn't ask for any of this! I only went drama cause you did and I wanted to copy you cause you were my hero. And when I got picked for the show I thought you'd be impressed and let me play with you and not be mean to me. I texted you the day you opened your salon and said I was so proud of you and asked you to do my nails and you never replied. You talk about America? I hated it! Do you know what my happiest time was? When we went to Fuengirola as a family and no fucker knew who I was and I got to be who I'd always wanted to be, just a normal kid and your sister. You talk about awards? My proudest moment ever weren't no award, it was on that holiday when that Spanish lad, Jose, nicked my fishing net and you battered him and went 'no one fucks with my sister!' Do you know how proud I was? I was walking ten foot tall that you stuck up for me. That meant more than any fucking award. You don't wanna be Natasha's sister so bad but I wanna be Sophie's sister so bad. I am so happy you've met Rob but I am so jealous. He loves you for being you. Not cause you were in a TV show, not cause you sold some records, not in case you've got money. You talk about Kelly's your maid of honour cause she's a good mate to ya, I don't have any mates! I never have, just users who want to sell stories to the papers about me or want to get in clubs for free. But everyone knows me though don't they? They *love* me, they *hate* me, they're *worried* about me, they're *angry* with me. THEY DON'T, EVEN, FUCKING, KNOW ME!!"

Then she screamed, several times, high-pitched and loud. She walked backwards into the corner of the room. Then her strength went. She leaned against the wall and slid down it so she was sitting on the ground, still with her head in her hands, and still crying hysterically. "I won't come to your wedding and wreck it I won't come to your wedding and wreck it I won't come to your wedding and wreck it I won't..."

Sophie, who looked concerned and not angry anymore, rushed over to the corner of the room and pulled Natasha's hands from her face. "Tasha, hey, calm down Tasha." she said it in a caring way. Like a big sister.

Natasha looked up with tears streaming down her cheeks, "You really don't want me there Soph, you mean it?"

"Of course I want you there. I won't get married if you ain't there. I need you there. I didn't mean that stuff I'm just, I don't know, I'm just still a bit mad at Mum and Dad about a lot of stuff but I don't hate you Tasha, I don't want you to think that, I love you, the *real* you. And I'll never let no fucker steal your fishing net."

That made Natasha giggle even though she was still sort of crying. "Thanks Soph."

"Wait there Tasha I'll get us a drink." She picked up her phone and went into the kitchen for what seemed like ages. When she came back she opened a new bottle of wine and refilled their glasses.

"One thing I said was true though Tasha. Kelly is a great mate, she's the sort of mate you can text the night before your wedding to tell that you're having your sister as maid of honour and she totally understands. That's a mate, she'll be a great bridesmaid though."

"You should have your best mate as maid of honour Soph."

"I agree with ya. And my best mate happens to be my annoying little sister. What you say? Will you do it?"

Natasha nodded her head and cried again. Sophie hugged her in a protective way and kissed her head

"Thank you Sophie, I'm dead proud."

"One thing though Tasha. Kane is innocent isn't he?"

"Don't worry about the trial man this is your wedding tomorrow."

"I need to know Tasha, so I can enjoy tomorrow."

"Course he is. He was with me that night."

They hugged for ages then Sophie tried her dress on. Natasha had never seen anyone look that beautiful before. She looked like a princess. Then they got drunk and talked about old holidays and stuff when they were kids. And they both laughed for hours. It was the best night of her life so far.

Natasha had never cried so much and she'd never been this happy.

Chapter 18

THREE WEEKS LATER SHE was sitting on her bed in her flat staring into space and chewing her hair when she got the call. There was no point ignoring it. "What do you want Kane?" she sounded flat and defeated.

"You know what I want. It's dat time of the week again. But I'm gonna need three grand this time." he sounded cheerful.

"I ain't got it."

"Don't lie. You ain't in court now you know! I know MC Booya bootlegged your track and I know for a fact they're paying you for it, why you lying for?"

"Please Kane."

"Don't come dat sweet little innocent girl ting with me. Pay me innit!"

"No Kane. I won't."

"Oh well in dat case I better get off the phone cause man have to ring your sister's husband innit? Tell him he married a slag. Cheating on her hen weekend, he´s gonna be vexed"

"She was off her face! She woke up in a hotel and knew she'd had sex but no idea who with. She probably had her drink spiked! She was probably raped! I told you that in confidence Kane, cause I loved ya and I trusted ya. How can you use this to blackmail me Kane? How?"

"I use what I need to use. Three grand ain't nuttin' to you anyway."

"I ain't giving ya no more money Kane. Rob won't believe you anyway. So you're wasting your time."

"Maybe. I tink he will believe me though, and dat's your sister's marriage over. And even if he don't, she'll know it's true and she'll know you must've told me so dat's her hating you for life, you're fucked either way." He'd got her there.

One last try, "You said if I lied for you in court, if I said you was with me that night that you wouldn't say nothing about Sophie on her hen. You promised me Kane, and I did it. I lied for you. I lied for you!"

"Dat's another ting, how's it gonna look for you if I declare dat?"

"You'd get life in jail you idiot."

"I'm gonna get life in jail at some point anyway. Prison don't mean shit to me. You though? You gonna be licking pussy in there like a bitch while your family sit around crying. Three grand Tasha yeah? And my lips seal up."

There was no point in arguing with him. "OK Kane. OK. I'll pay. Where shall we meet? Same alley?"

"You know dat! Also I need you to bring me my ting."

"What thing?"

"Don't be a dickhead. My strap. It's taped up in the base of the sofa. Be careful it's loaded."

"I'll bring it. I don't want it in my house anyway."

"I don't give a fuck what you want! See you at two. Later." Then he hung up.

She felt so tired. This was never going to stop. Natasha tried to think of her options. She could kill herself, but then he might still ruin Sophie's life. She suddenly felt completely exhausted. She fell on her bed, grabbed her pillow tightly and sobbed and sobbed.

Chapter 19

FIVE HOURS LATER KANE was waiting in the alley when she got there, he looked impatient.

"You got my tings?" He sounded pretty aggressive.

Natasha pulled the handgun out of her bag and pointed it at Kane. "I'm not giving you no more money."

"Who da fuck you tink you are? Don't point dat at me! Give me dat now or I'll slap you up!"

Kane walked towards Natasha. Natasha shot him three times and Kane dropped to the ground. Dead.

Natasha then fell to her knees and dropped the gun. Sobbing hysterically she said, "You can't threaten my sister no more. No one fucks with my sister!"

A glamorous looking woman in an expensive dress walked out the shadows. She was pretty and looked a bit Spanish.

"Well that was unexpected!" said the woman, cheerfully.

"Are you the police?" asked Natasha. The woman actually seemed to think for a second as if she wasn't sure.

"Kind of! I think of us as the police. We're my police. We're not the proper old bill police though, I can't arrest you if that's what you're worried about."

"What have I done?" Then in almost a whisper as it began to sink in, she repeated, "What have I done?"

"Dropped a gun with your fingerprints on it for one thing. Silly! Come on, give it to me and come with me. We need to get out of here." said the woman, pulling Natasha up to her feet by her arm and leading her out the alley to a car.

As she did this she took the gun off Natasha and made a phone call. When she hung up she took the SIM card out of the phone and dropped it down a drain. She got in the driving seat and Natasha got in the front and they drove off. Natasha was sobbing and sucking her thumb which she hadn't done since she was a child.

The phone call the woman had made had been short and very confusing. Maybe she'd phoned the police and was driving Natasha to custody.

"What was that about a river?" asked Natasha which was the only bit of the call she'd heard.

"Never you mind. I've claimed responsibility for the shooting that's all you need to know. You're welcome by the way."

"Are the police gonna be looking for me?"

"No they're going to be looking for me! Well me and my friends anyway."

"How come you've done that?"

"You ask a lot of questions! I think it's me who should be asking the questions! Why did you kill him?"

"He was blackmailing me."

That made the woman laugh. "Blackmail? That's funny, that's what the papers will call him till they find out who he is. How ironic! What was he blackmailing you about? Was he forcing you to listen to that remix of *World In Motion* you did when you were a kid in the World Cup or Euros or whatever it was, where you rapped with John Barnes? Cause that was fucking annoying by the way!"

Of all the bad reviews she'd ever got this was definitely the strangest. "No he knew stuff. He threatened to tell secret stuff. I weren't gonna shoot him just threaten him. I thought he'd be scared and leave me alone. But he weren't and he came at me, you saw!" This was true. That was exactly what had happened. Maybe this woman could be a witness for her in court.

"Well he'll definitely leave you alone now. Come on stop crying will you? God you're even more annoying in real life! Close your eyes and go to your happy place or something."

"My happy place? That would be Fuengirola."

"What's funky roller?"

"Fuengirola it's on the Costa Del Sol in Spain. We used to go on holiday there when I was a little kid. I'm gonna go there now I think, clear my head."

"Good choice! I'll drive you to the airport. We'll go to your flat first so you can pick up your stuff, I'll lose this gun and phone on the way."

Natasha continued sobbing and sucking her thumb till they arrived at the airport. Then the woman said, "Go on, get out, go to Fuengirola and lie low and NEVER tell anyone what you did. You got enough to cash to live out there for a while?"

Natasha nodded. "I don't know how to thank you. What's your name by the way? You know mine."

"Leah. If I ever need you I know where to find you don't I? Go on, get out."

She got out. Three months later Leah arrived in Spain. They never mentioned that night again.

Chapter 20

"TASHA YOU KNOW *Nat's life*?" asked Dave and it took her a second to remember where she was.

"Was that the reggae cover of *That's Life* you did? I remember that!" said Jamie and then sung reggae style,

"Nat's life. Dat's what all dem people say. Do your maths and English homework, but man I just wanna play!"

"Please don't do that." said Natasha.

"Well I've written some bars and I'm gonna sample the chorus. Check it" said Dave and then he rapped. "Her name's Natasha and I wanna smash her, up the anus, she is pretty famous, all these bitches know what my name is-"

"You're going to sing about shagging her and sample her as a child in the chorus?" interrupted Taylor.

"Errr you dirty bwoy!" said Jamie in Dave's accent.

"It's better than the original! No offence Tasha." said Leah with a smile.

"Frank Sinatra did the original. Moron." snapped Jess.

"You know people in the music business Tasha, you must know someone who'll sign me as a rapper what?" said Dave looking at her hopefully.

"I don't know anyone who can help ya."

"What you don't know no one in the music business?"

"I didn't say that." As Natasha said this Jamie burst out laughing

"Maybe you're better as an underground artist?" said Jess trying to help.

"Nah. I wanna blow up mainstream. Earn the dollars."

Natasha suddenly had an idea. "Thing is Dave you're a gangster ain't ya? And you're known as Stone Cold. If you get famous they'll know who you are and they can catch you for all your crimes can't they?"

Dave leapt off his chair with excitement. "Dis is why I need to marry dis gal! Spot on Tasha! I need to marry you innit, you're on my level!"

Jess smiled at her and Jamie said "Let´s get another round. What ya having Tasha?"

Natasha smiled. "Got any crack?" Leah, Jamie, Jess and Taylor all burst out laughing and Leah clinked Natasha's glass. Natasha felt at home. She really loved this group.

Part 4

UNDER PRESSURE: TAYLOR
'When Her World Falls Down She Won't Crumble, Under Pressure.'

Chapter 21

PEOPLE SAID SHE GOT her toughness from her dad. It wasn't true. What was tough about him? He didn't face things, he escaped from them. It's what he was famous for. He'd escaped from the responsibility of getting a job by walking into banks and building societies and more specifically, security vans with a gun and stealing money. Then he'd escaped from risking his life doing that by investing in drug deals, then he'd escaped going down by running to Spain and then Cyprus. He'd escaped being a dad too really, Taylor didn't care that he didn't really stay in touch with her but the fact he didn't bother with Dave upset her. He'd escaped being a grandad too. He'd never even met Bennie. Her mum didn't escape though. Her mum faced things. Her mum faced the reporters, neighbours and police, her mum had faced the rival dealers who'd broken into their house, her mum had faced helping Taylor hear again after the shotgun blast ruptured her eardrums, and her mum had faced being a mum and now a nanny. Taylor always faced things too. She got her toughness from her mum. And she was very, very proud of that.

Today she'd faced Dennis. She had to. He'd been outside Gloria's when she left and had walked with her. She'd agreed to go for a coffee with him. Being short and snappy with him hadn't worked. She'd been trying that since he arrived and he didn't appear to be in the least bit put off by it, so she'd had a long hard think and realised that it was best not to show him any emotion at all. She'd worked in sales long enough to know that. She'd been taught that emotion is usually temporary, no one stays angry or happy or sad or whatever for any length of time unless they're mentally ill. In her old sales job she'd never minded if a client was angry, you could work with that. Her old colleague Gary used to say that while they were emotional, they were engaged, and how it was impossible to feel emotion and not care but if a client was calm and happy to talk but had found a new supplier then that was that, then she knew she'd lost that account. So over the coffee she was polite and friendly if a little distant. She wanted to show Dennis that she wouldn't calm down, that she was already calm and not angry with him anymore. That she wasn't emotionally engaged. That he'd lost that account.

Dennis however wasn't having any of it. He simply adjusted himself to the conversation and adapted accordingly. So where as previously he'd been periodically nipping into Gloria's bar and declaring his love for Taylor to the world with a happy smile and demeanor to counter her toxic frostiness, now he sat there sipping his cappuccino and telling her very matter of factly how much he adored her, he said all this as calmly as if he'd been telling her that it was half past four. But two extremely important things had occurred during this coffee meeting, which gave Taylor a great deal to think about. For one thing, Dennis had slipped up.

She'd told him how she was looking forward to going out with the girls on Friday night to the strip. This was a trap and although he hadn't risen to it and had told her it was great, fantastic, etc and said he'd love to take care of Bennie that night and get to know him again, he'd said how much he'd missed Bennie and that was when it happened. She'd told him that Jamie was taking care of him, and he'd said that was weird, that Jamie was a childless man who she hardly knew and as a mother she had to put Bennie first. And as he was doing his best to convince her that Jamie was a dangerous pedophile, he'd said 'I mean, why is he so interested in you? Why not Leah or one of the others?' He was of course trying to imply that the attraction was Bennie and though the suggestion that Jamie was a child abuser was laughable, and Taylor wasn't going to be manipulated by such nastiness, surely he'd broken character here.

If you loved someone so much that you were obsessed enough to follow them to Spain and they were the most beautiful woman in the world and all the rest of it, why would you question why someone else would be interested in them? You wouldn't would you? If you felt for example that the two most beautiful women you'd ever seen in your life were Taylor blonde and Taylor brunette, then surely you wouldn't assume that any normal person would rather have Leah and that there must be an ulterior and sinister motive to want Taylor instead. This was important because it showed her, *proved* to her that she wasn't mad. She'd been beginning to doubt that lately. Sometimes she stood in front of the mirror and repeated to her reflection 'You're not mad' a gesture which contradicted itself if you thought about it. But she had proof now. In the sanity hearing that regularly took place within her own head, the defence now had a powerful piece of evidence. She knew that Dennis marketed himself well and her new friends in Spain all thought she was being unreasonable to him and she understood why. How could she of all people judge them for falling for him? And she never spoke badly of him to them, partly because she was embarrassed, any criticism of him was surely a reflection on her as she'd been with him for over two years. It was like those people who slag off a job that they've been at for years and tell you how bad they get treated there, you come away feeling that all they've really told you is that they're a mug who puts up with crap all day and allows themselves to be bullied cause they're too scared or weak to walk away. It reflects far more badly on them than it does on the company they work for.

The other important thing was that Dennis claimed to have had a conversation with Leah and Jess where they'd asked him if Taylor was smuggling drugs in Bennie's teddy bears and Dennis claimed to have got the impression that Jamie had put that idea in their heads. He said he'd put them straight and told them it was nonsense. Taylor really didn't want to believe that but the time he said this happened was the exact time Jamie was accusing her of it. Would he really have done that? She hoped not, but she couldn't see any other explanation. She really hoped it wasn't true because the truth was that she really, really liked Jamie. Now a bit of a question mark hung over him. She was already a bit confused as she wasn't sure what, if anything, was happening with Jamie.

She'd gone round for their usual weekly wine and board games night after her coffee with Dennis. She'd sort of hoped it was going to be the night things happened, but Jamie hadn't made a move. He'd told her she looked great, that was the exact sentence he used, but 'you look great' is what you say to an aunt who's had cancer or something and has just finished her treatment and started growing her hair back, not really what you'd say if you were struggling to resist the urge to jump on someone. Her and Jamie had got really close recently, she'd never spent any time alone with any of the others in the group, unless you counted the time she went shopping with Natasha, or the fact that she gave the girls makeovers, (except Jess of course who wouldn't touch anything tested on animals) but her and Jamie were spending more and more time together, and wine and board games night had become a weekly event that she really looked forward to, and the more she got to know him, the more she liked him.

They seemed to have this connection where when they discussed their past or their opinions or whatever, just as much was unsaid as was said, and what was unsaid was just as loud and as clear and as understood and agreed with by them both as anything they said out loud. It was as if they had two parallel conversations running simultaneously in complete alignment. She'd never had this kind of closeness with anyone before where it seemed as if their subconsciouses talked to each other in secret, and got on with each other just as well as their conscious selves did. Jamie was like a good book. The type of book that started off nice and easy to read and then took a bit of a twist and suddenly you realised it was layered with hidden depth, and you started to look forward to reading it, and you liked every chapter, then every paragraph, then every line, and before you knew it you were hooked. Taylor had always liked books. As a child she'd been a bit of an introvert and had always loved reading. Once when she was about twenty, her and her mum had spent four hundred pounds between them on books and stayed in quietly reading for weeks. One of the problems her passion for literature had caused was that she couldn't tolerate bad spelling. The first boyfriend she ever thought she loved was Callum McDonough who she'd gone out with when they were in year ten and she'd texted him to tell him that she'd fallen in love with him and he'd texted back 'I love you to' she'd dumped him the next day. It wasn't as if she was being unreasonable, she'd already ignored the fact he said 'could of'. There was only so much she could take.

• • • •

THE NEXT DAY SHE WAS in Gloria's bar with Jamie, Leah, Jess and Natasha. She'd tried to ignore it but it was like it was glaring at her, she thought if she just pointed it out to the others one of them would deal with it but they didn't, they weren't outraged by it at all. Not even Jamie, and he knew it was wrong, instead he just said, "I don't see why it matters. You know what it means."

"Cause it's spelt wrong."

Natasha looked confused, "I don't understand. Ain't it called expresso?"

"No! It's espresso!" Taylor realised she was barking at Natasha like a German in a black and white war film so she softened her tone a bit and smiled, "There's no x in it."

"What about you Taylor?" asked Leah smiling, "had an ex in you recently?"

"What do you mean by that?!"

"You and Dennis went out yesterday didn't you? I saw Dave, he was *so* excited. He thinks you're getting back together."

Dave hadn't seen them so Dennis had obviously told him. Great. "We went for a coffee. That's it. Then I went to Jamie's for our wine and board games night."

"You two have a wine and board games night?" asked Jess who looked really upset and hurt. Maybe she wanted to be invited.

"We have a couple of times. Don't think we'll be playing Cluedo again though, Taylor seems to think you can appeal the verdict if you lose." said Jamie.

Taylor had explained to Jamie at the time what was so stupid about the game and decided to test her theory on the group.

"It's ridiculous! If it was the revolver everyone would have heard it! Are you telling me that Colonel Mustard, who must have spent years in the military to reach his rank, doesn't know a gunshot when he hears one? It would have been deafening. If it was Reverend Green in the study with the revolver, and Colonel Mustard never mentioned hearing a firearm discharge when he was interviewed by detectives then he's involved. Trust me."

Jamie pointed out that was the reason he wouldn't play Cluedo with her again. Then Gloria arrived with a tray of drinks.

Before she could stop herself, she'd said it, "Gloria sorry to be an annoying bitch but it's 'espresso'." It just slipped out. Taylor knew at this point that there was no such thing as time travel, or at least that she herself would never acquire a time machine because future Taylor would have come in at that moment and prevented the awkward conversation. Although thinking about it future Taylor probably wouldn't have time, she'd be much too busy preventing some of the more serious fuck ups.

"Sorry I thought you said you wanted a white wine! I'll change it."

"No, I do want a white wine but, it's espresso."

"No it's not it's wine. How can wine be coffee?"

She wished she hadn't said anything. "No I mean, you've written expresso on the board. It's actually espresso. No 'x'." She smiled as she said it and tried to sound helpful but she knew she sounded rude or possibly mental.

"Have you got OCD Taylor?" asked Leah happily.

"Maybe. A little bit." admitted Taylor.

"How come you can spell so good Taylor?" asked Natasha

"I read a lot."

Natasha looked puzzled, "About coffee?"

"No! Just in general."

"Do you have to read the same book over and over again or your family will die?" asked Leah looking delighted.

"OCD's nothing to laugh at Leah." snapped Jess "It can be a horrible thing to have."

"God! You leftist hippies don't laugh at anything do you? Well except Christianity and British culture and stuff, politically correct giggles."

As Leah said this Taylor saw her window.

"Are you sure you two don't have OCD? You both seem to have to have a political debate every three minutes. You're never going to agree and you're never going to change each other's views so what's the point?"

This was true but she didn't really mind the political debates. They were interesting and both Jess and Leah often made good points. The truth was that Taylor just wanted to change the subject from her spelling OCD.

"Take a bow Taylor. That was the most intelligent thing that's been said at this table for ages!" said Jamie, laughing.

"Cause she reads. That's why she's so smart man." remarked Natasha, looking at Taylor almost in awe.

"Yeah I wish I was smart like Taylor. Then I could be a single mum from Rochdale." As Leah said this Taylor almost laughed. Leah probably owed her a snipe and to be fair that was a good one.

Gloria understandably looked quite uncomfortable.

"I think I'll get back behind the bar on that note. Oh before I do, I need you guys to give me your passports to make copies of. Don't matter if you haven't got them now, but I'll need them ASAP."

"How come?" asked Jess.

"Spanish authorities get funny if we don't check and keep a note. Can cause havoc with my licence and you lot are here all the time. I'll need Bennie's as well Taylor."

"Really? He's not over eighteen if that's what he's told you."

Gloria laughed. "He seems happy enough with Oreo cakes rather than beer for now so he hasn't tried that yet, but on a serious one, I will need it. Just bring them next time you guys are in yeah?" Then she went back behind the bar.

Taylor felt this was an unusual request. Why would she need their passports? "That's weird. She needs copies of all our passports. Even Bennie's?"

"Not that weird when you think about it." said Jamie. "You know what the Spanish authorities are like. Remember all the hassle you have to go through just to get an NIE number and social security so you can actually pay them tax? Not that I pay much considering I hardly earn anything."

Jess nodded in agreement. "I earn much less than I did in the UK, but the cost of living's so cheap here that I'm actually a lot richer. How much would you need to earn in England to get an apartment with a balcony and swimming pool? And I absolutely *love* my job! What about you Taylor? Did you earn more in the UK than you do working for yourself here?"

That would be a massive understatement.

"A lot more. But as you say it's about quality of life."

"You and Bennie have a better quality of life here I take it?"

That of course would be the biggest understatement of all.

Chapter 22

SEVEN MONTHS AGO, CHELMSFORD, Essex

Taylor was having a cigarette with her colleague Gary. She was smartly dressed and her natural coloured shoulder-length dark hair was slightly crimped. They were standing at the end of the car park near the pavement which was where you had to go to smoke. Gary was the same age as her but looked a lot younger. For one thing he was quite short and Taylor always felt that he looked like a naughty kid from an old comic-book from the nineteen-thirties. Despite the fact he was wearing a suit and had his short brown hair neatly parted, he still looked like he should be wearing an old-fashioned school cap and stuffing his blazer pockets with jammy dodgers whilst giggling to himself.

Taylor and Gary got on well. They'd joined the company at the same time and were still the two newest members of staff (even though they were both regularly top of the sales board) and although they'd joined in a batch of six or seven newbies, they were the two who were made permanent. Part of the reason that Taylor was doing so well was because she'd listened to and learned from Gary. Despite appearances he was highly intelligent and had an instinctive understanding of human psychology which helped in sales. Taylor wasn't too fussed on most of the others in the office, they were, it had to be said, a boring bunch and seemed incapable of talking about anything other than work. Gary talked about work too but he did it in a humorous way, he had Taylor's dark sense of humour and although people always said that you should make friends with people who like the same things as you, what made Gary and Taylor so close was, they *hated* the same things as each other, and as Taylor realised that was the basis of a meaningful friendship.

Gary was always smiling and always looked like he was about to burst out laughing, except today. Today he seemed a bit distant and looked like he was in his own world. Taylor was still buzzing about the phone call she'd just had and was taking deep adrenaline fuelled pulls on her cigarette. She was telling Gary about the call but he didn't seem to be listening and was just staring straight ahead so she stopped talking and tried to see what was distracting him. Maybe she wasn't explaining it clearly enough? She did worry about that. Sometimes there appeared to be no correlation between her thoughts and her speech. Her thoughts were concise and well laid out like chairs round a posh table at an aristocratic wedding, yet when she spoke she felt like she sort of barked out the words, as if a gang of hooligans had gate crashed the aristocratic couple's reception and were hurling the chairs randomly out of her mouth at an unseen foe. It just came out wrong, like how everyone thinks they can sing until they try out loud in front of people. She looked around to see what might have got his attention or upset him. There wasn't much to look at, a Romanian looking bloke in a forklift truck unloading a lorry in the warehouse next door, a father and son gardening in a house opposite, she decided to carry on with her story.

"Then he goes 'but I can get this a lot cheaper elsewhere.' Now Gary you know this is my biggest client. This account's going put Bennie through uni! I'm shitting myself, so really calm I said, 'Andrew I don't doubt you can, but this is for your clients, and we're the best. It might cost more but would you rather your clients felt like they had the best or the cheapest?' He went quiet for what seemed like two hundred years but I remembered what you taught me. First one to speak loses, so I'm silent and I'm shitting myself and I can hear my own heart beat and he goes. 'Yeah, go on Taylor we'll do it with your company again.'"

"Cool."

"I am *so* fucking happy I can't tell you."

"Yeah."

He hadn't even looked at her once, he was just staring straight ahead. "Gary are you OK? It's just you seem really weird with me today."

Now Gary looked at her. He looked quite serious which didn't really suit him, he was clearly upset about something.

"Fuck it, I'm just gonna say this. I just don't get you at all Taylor. I thought we were mates and I think you're so funny and I have such a laugh working with you. You crack me up with your crazy rants. But we're not mates are we?"

What the fuck was he on about? "What do you mean? Of course we are."

"Yeah? Every week when we go for a drink after work I invite you, and every week you have a different excuse why you can't come."

"I have a two and half year-old child! I can't always go to the pub just like that. I thought you understood that."

"I know you do. That's why I tried to tag you in this thing on Facebook yesterday. Just some silly thing about how babies are like old people cause they're bald and wrinkly and whinge if they don't get their own way. But I couldn't tag you could I? Cause you've deleted me. Not sure what I've ever done wrong to you."

"I didn't delete you, I didn't! It must have been an accident or something."

Gary snorted and raised his eyebrows. "Yeah an accident. Taylor if you don't wanna be mates that's fine. Just don't make it awkward yeah?"

Then he flicked his half smoked cigarette onto the pavement and walked back in the office.

Taylor stared at the cigarette smoldering on the ground. If she'd deleted Gary off her Facebook, she'd obviously done it by accident and he'd clearly overreacted but she didn't want to fall out with or upset him. She knew what she had to do, even though it was probably going to lead to an argument. She stamped out his cigarette with the heel of her shoe and walked back into the office.

Gary was pacing up and down on his headset with his back to the door so he didn't see her approach him. "I don't care if he's in a meeting! Go and get him.... No. I'll speak to him now, thank you..... How long have you been his PA?.... OK well I've managed his account for years so go fetch him.... You must be stunning looking cause you haven't been hired for your brain have you?.. Listen to me, if he misses out on this offer cause you didn't put my call through he'll-"

Taylor pressed the button on Gary's phone which hung up the call. "You're going to the pub tonight right?"

Gary looked shocked. "Fuck's sake Taylor you just hung up on my best client!"

"Don't care. Yes or no?"

"Yeah there's a few of us going. The usual lot."

"And me. If that's OK?"

Gary beamed a smile at her. "You know you're always welcome."

"I'll be there. If you buy me a drink I might add you on Facebook"

He laughed and said, "And if you buy me one I might accept your friend request."

Ali who was their boss, opened the door to his office and leaned out onto the sales floor. "Taylor can I have a quick word in my office please?" he said, sounding friendly.

Taylor cringed, mouthed 'oh shit' to Gary who sympathetically cringed back and then she walked into Ali's office and sat down opposite him.

The office had a window which overlooked the car park where they smoked. On the desk was a large signed photo of the Arsenal team which had a plaque that said 'Invincibles 03/04' and several tenpin bowling trophies which Ali had won, most of which had jokes alluding to the fact that he was called Ali and that bowling traditionally takes place in an alley.

Ali was in his mid thirties, he was fat and had a neat box beard and was wearing a shirt and tie, he looked like a sort of Asian Ricky Gervais. Taylor liked Ali, he had family in Rochdale and although when she first learned that she'd panicked in case he connected her with her family, he didn't seem to make the connection and just seemed keen to discuss the area with her. Although he'd spent his whole life in Essex, he had a faint Indian accent. He was a kind boss. His only fault was he had an annoying habit of ending a sentence with 'innit' and then immediately correcting it with 'isn't it' even when neither was correct. For example, 'you've already hit your target innit? Sorry I mean you've already hit your target isn't it?' And she wanted to scream 'No! You've already hit your target HAVEN'T YOU? You thicko!' To her eternal credit however she had resisted the urge to do that so far which was probably how she still had her job.

She decided to pre-empt the conversation. "If this is about me hanging up Gary's call, I didn't realise he was on the phone to his client. I'm really sorry."

Ali looked surprised. "You hung up one of Gary's calls? I wouldn't worry about that, that boy will probably get us closed down one of these days with how rude he is. Still, he is a great salesman and smashes his target, he's just been a right menace since he watched that *Wolf of Wall Street!*"

Taylor laughed and relaxed, "So what's this about?"

Ali went on to explain how this wasn't a criticism, how her scores were through the roof and that a lot of the lads didn't like being beaten by a girl and had therefore upped their scores which was great for the company.

"I listened to one of your calls earlier and how you handled that client was brilliant. Most of that lot out there would've lost that account but you didn't panic and you handled it superb. I'm gonna play that call in tomorrow's meeting if you don't mind?"

Taylor smiled nervously, "Yeah I don't mind, I'll just sit there cringing, wishing I was dead."

Ali burst out laughing. "Just one quick thing before you go back, I know that you and Gary and some of the others mess about and have banter, I really don't care. You and Gary have both hit your target for this month already, so if you wanna have a laugh and mess about a bit, that's fine with me. It shows the rest of that lot that when they hit target we relax on them as a company but the only thing Taylor is, you can't go on Facebook in the day, just breaks and lunch yeah?"

Now Taylor was very confused, "I haven't been."

Ali smiled. "I can see how you do so well here, you're a great saleswoman but you've forgotten the golden rule. Never accept your boss' friend request! I can see when you're online and you were online this morning before break, innit? *Isn't it?*"

"Ali, I wasn't!" She was sure she wasn't. One day she hoped she'd be able to go ten minutes without arguing about what she had or hadn't done on Facebook.

Ali looked a bit disappointed with her. "It's not a big deal, just from now on yeah? Go on, get back out there and show that lot how it's done."

If Taylor thought these two incidents were unconnected then three hours later she realised they were anything but.

Chapter 23

SHE WAS IN HER FLAT putting on make-up in the mirror. She could see Dennis' reflection, he was sitting in an armchair watching her. This was before he got his scar so his face was more symmetrical and his eyes were drilling her through the mirror, watching her every move the way a shopping centre security guard watches a teenage hoodie. She waited for the inevitable and as she was applying the finishing touches to her mascara it happened. And it started pretty much how she expected it would.

"I'm just asking cause I can't understand this. You've seen them all day, why do you have to go back out with them now?"

"Please don't start Dennis. I'm only going out for an hour."

"I'm not *starting*, I'm asking you to explain it Tay, so I can understand it, why won't you answer the question?"

"I'm just going to have a laugh and a chat with some people I work with, that's all."

She'd been repeating that statement in her head all afternoon, as she knew this would happen and she had to remind herself that she was doing nothing wrong, because she knew that Dennis would probably make her feel like she was, and it was important she kept herself sane because he could be extremely convincing and she could sort of go under from the weight of his argument. If you're in court it doesn't really matter whether you're innocent or guilty does it? It matters whether your lawyer is better at arguing than their lawyer. Dennis would have made a good lawyer.

"It don't add up Tay. You see them all day. You have lunch and fag breaks with them. What I don't get is what can't you talk to them about then that you want to talk about with them now?"

In fact Dennis bombarded her with messages in her lunch hour and if she didn't respond immediately he'd message her a load of question marks so as a consequence she spent her entire lunch hour responding to his messages which made her appear rude and unsociable and therefore no one except Gary bothered to try and talk to her. She decided not to mention that and stuck to the battle she was fighting.

"Oh god! I don't know exactly what we're going to talk about! Why does it have to be like this every time I go out?"

"Cause you're being secretive."

"No I'm not!"

"Yes you are. You're hiding something and you're avoiding questions. A couple of weeks ago when we visited your brother in Spain we got on great. Soon as we're back you can't wait to go out with god knows who till fuck knows when."

"I'm going out for one hour Dennis, with the work lot. And yes we had a great time in Spain but it's not me who's different there it's you, and it's because you're more relaxed cause Dave isn't a threat to you cause he's my brother."

She said this in a really calm and soothing voice and smiled at him gently as she said it, as she genuinely thought he might realise she was right, but it backfired, he looked angrier than ever, and his anger had a look of justified righteousness, as if he'd caught her out.

"Well that clears it up. Now we're getting somewhere. Who's a threat to me here?"

"No one! But you think people are. Men anyway."

"You said Dave's *not* a threat. You didn't say I don't *see* him as a threat. See what I mean? That means *you* think someone is, not me. Who is it Taylor? Who are you fucking? Or planning to?"

Was it even worth all this just to go for a drink which she didn't really want to go for anyway? Probably not but she was in the right and she had to show Dennis that he wasn't being reasonable as it had been getting worse and worse lately and this situation was starting to become unbearable.

"This is crazy! I'm going out for one hour! With a whole group of people!"

"Gary will be there I take it? And don't even think about lying."

"I don't need to lie! Yes he's going. So what? It's not just me and him. And anyway for the millionth time he's just a friend..." Taylor suddenly stopped doing her makeup. She felt despair in the pit of her stomach and also a touch of anger as the realisation set in. She turned away from the mirror and faced Dennis.

"Dennis. Did you delete Gary off my Facebook?" She knew the answer already of course.

Dennis leapt from his chair and stormed over to her. "Who Gary? Innocent friend Gary? The one who calls you 'naughty sausage' in his messages?"

"That's a joke! I told you about that! An old posh client who's seventy-five years old called me a naughty sausage and Gary and the others thought it was hilarious and now they all call me it to take the piss! You shouldn't be logging onto my account and reading my messages. I got in trouble at work today because they thought I was online and it's obviously you logging on. I'll show you all my messages from everyone, I don't have anything to hide. You don't need to log on and delete people."

"Who else did I delete?"

"What?"

"I deleted Gary but who else? You noticed Gary."

Oh god. How would she know without checking? It could be any male really and she had about three hundred friends. She'd probably never know unless he told her.

"I don't know Dennis I haven't checked."

He grabbed her very roughly by her face pushing his thumb and fingers into her cheeks and slammed her head against the wall. He continued to squeeze her face painfully hard, his hand covering her mouth, as he screamed at her, his face contorted with rage.

"Me! I deleted myself! But you don't notice that do you? No but you clock that Gary's gone straight away! That's why I did it. To see who you'd notice was missing first. Me or him! Do you know something Taylor? You're fucking ugly! That's why you need that make-up cause you're a fucking dog. He's only interested in you cause you're a slag, an easy shag. Couldn't even keep your legs closed on a girls holiday to Magaluf, ended up with a kid cause you let a stranger fuck you. You don't even know your kid's dad's name! That's what you're like. A dirty ugly whore who lets anyone up her cunt! I'd love to see this Gary support your kid and take him on like I have! You bag of sick. You don't know how lucky are! Your face actually makes me wanna puke. You're vile, once he's shagged you he'll leave you. You'll be all alone, no one else would put up with you. Your own dad took one look at you and walked out. You ended up a deaf mong cause of him and he still doesn't send you any money even though he's a millionaire gangster, he doesn't even call to see how you are. He chose to take that retard of a brother of yours with him rather than you, that's how fucking annoying you are. You couldn't even kill yourself properly. You even failed at that! That's how pathetic you are. I'm the only person that'd put up with you. Do you know something? You're an ugly, stupid, fucking...."

Chapter 24

OBVIOUSLY BENNIE HAD a much better quality of life in Spain. Taylor knew that of course, what was of great concern was she didn't know how long she could sustain it for. The makeup business she was running was a con really, it was essentially a pyramid scheme where she was having to pay so much back that she hardly made a profit. She'd come up with the rather ingenious idea of doing makeovers as well as selling the actual makeup which had massively increased her income but there was only really Gloria, Natasha and Leah and one or two others, how often would they need makeovers? Her savings were pretty much done now. She was so worried she hadn't slept properly for days. How come things like this never happened to people like Dennis? How come he could just stroll off a plane and into a well paid, secure job while people like her struggled? She decided to just try and enjoy her time with her friends today and relax. She'd have a good think later. She'd work out what the problem was and then she'd fix it.

"Yeah must be well better for Bennie to grow up here near the beach rather than Rochdale. No offence Taylor." said Natasha.

"We lived in Essex before we moved here but yeah. Still much better for him here." said Taylor, truthfully.

"Did you move to Essex when you met Dennis?" asked Jess.

"No I met him there. I moved there when I was pregnant."

"How come?" asked Natasha.

"Honestly? It's not easy to get a job in Rochdale with my surname and I wanted to work, wanted to set Bennie a good example."

"Well you do! exclaimed Jess smiling. "And as Tasha says it's a much better life for him here."

Taylor smiled at Jamie. "Well he *was* happy here. Till some idiot told him about Disneyland. Now he wants to live there and he hates it here cause it's 'a stupid wet poo' apparently."

"It's not my fault!" said Jamie laughing. "An advert for Disneyland came on the telly. He asked what it was. What could I do? I had to explain it to him."

"It's a made up place, it's where you go when you die. It's a horrid place where killers dressed as Disney characters murder children, loads of things you could have said. But no, you tell him the truth! Now he won't shut up about going there."

"I don't blame him I want to go there." said Leah sounding like a child.

"Really?" asked Jess sarcastically. "There's seven dwarfs there. Are dwarfs not on the list of people you hate?"

Leah smiled with delight. "Dwarfs? Oh that's an offensive word. I can't believe you called them that. That's a shame. For your information, they prefer the term *little people* Jess."

Natasha exploded with laughter. "She's got you there Jess! Who's got a fag by the way?"

As Jess was the only one of their group who didn't smoke the question probably wasn't directed at her but she answered it anyway. "Obviously not me cause I'm proud to not be a slave to the tobacco companies. Although from the amount of passive shit I breathe from the rest of you I may as well smoke."

"Have you never smoked Jess?" asked Jamie.

"Yeah. Till I learned how the tobacco industry has no regard for human suffering. I used to really enjoy it to be honest."

"I couldn't quit even if I wanted to, which I don't. It's one of the only fun things I can afford. In fact my dream night which I am definitely going to do one night, is to get a pack of unfiltered retro, old school fags, a bottle of Jack Daniels and listen to Sinatra music all night. That would be so cool. A Frank Sinatra night." said Jamie enthusiastically.

"I couldn't quit. And I'm pretty good at quitting stuff! I probably would if I had a baby or something. Did you still smoke when you were pregnant Taylor?" asked Natasha.

"Believe it or not I started smoking when I was pregnant. Near the end."

Jess looked shocked. "Really?"

"I can imagine that. It must have been a stressful time." said Jamie sympathetically.

It had been of course. She'd been back from her holiday for two months without coming on when she took the test. She'd never been so frightened in her life. She'd thought about, well, you know, what women sometimes do when they're on their own with an unplanned pregnancy. But she'd quickly decided against it. She just couldn't do it, mainly because, even though she'd never had any desire to have a child, she'd felt an intense maternal bond and protective instinct towards Bennie straight away. It felt like there had always been part of her missing and she'd just never realised before what it was, but being pregnant somehow felt more natural to her than anything else had ever felt. She knew straight away that it was a boy and although she knew that it must be a trick of memory, she felt like she'd immediately pictured Bennie exactly how he looked now. But she was single and unemployed and she was a 'Seavers' so she'd decided to move to the bright lights of London. She was offered a job in Braintree in Essex (which had turned out to be a disaster) left Rochdale and then met Dennis.

Jamie knew very little of this or rather she'd told him very little of it, but the comment he'd just made about her smoking suggested he'd worked some of it out instinctively. Maybe they were just building such a strong bond. She found herself daydreaming about him quite a lot recently. Sometimes she'd look at how he was with Bennie and how happy Bennie was around him and she'd think about what a great dad he'd be. Other times she'd notice him looking at her in a way that made her think about, well, other stuff he might be good at.

"Anyway," he continued, "I'll go order the drinks. Help yourself to a fag out of my box Tasha."

Taylor felt it was a bit odd that he'd go to the bar to order their drinks as Gloria always served them at their table.

Chapter 25

"SMOOTH HOW I DID THAT with the passports right?" Gloria was smiling and she was right to. She'd done it brilliantly.

"Yeah it was brilliant. She did get a bit suspicious but she would, she's so clever, but I think I threw her off the scent." He hoped he had at any rate.

Gloria looked really excited. "So tell me what's happening!" she demanded.

"My old boss, he's in California now and I've got the chance to go and work there for six months, maybe longer. I'm gonna do it. I feel it's time to move on from here now. Career wise anyway."

"And you're going to ask Taylor to go with you?" asked Gloria inquisitively.

"Yeah, Bennie wants to go to Disneyland and we'd be right near. I know her brother lives here but she'd have a great life out there." Jamie had lied about an advert for Disneyland being on TV. He'd shown Bennie it on YouTube.

"You're not even going out with her! You haven't even kissed. I hope you're not heading for a knock back here."

Jamie understood her concern. He'd probably have said exactly the same thing if this was the other way round. But when you know, you know.

"There's something there. When it's just the two of us, or three of us with Bennie, we're like a family. I could make her happy. So yeah, I'm gonna surprise her with the flight tickets and see what she says. The worst thing she can say is no, and I never have to see the people here again so what does it matter?"

"Excuse me. We're family. You'll have to see me again, thank you very much. Oh speaking of family I was chatting to your mum last night."

"Yeah she said."

"You gonna go back and see her before you go?"

"Not while she's with that prick."

Gloria smiled affectionately and put her hand on his arm. "Oh yeah, so sorry Jamie, I had no idea what he was like before you told me. He always seemed such a nice guy."

Jamie looked at Taylor, "They always do don't they? In public. It's in private you see what they're really like."

Gloria nodded. "Yeah, your dad weren't great either though to be honest was he? How can a lovely woman like her always attract such wankers?"

"Not sure. I suppose when a woman's as amazing as her she just wants to see the best in people, wants to help them change into a better person, cause that's who she is, but they don't do they?" he said, still not taking his eyes off Taylor.

Chapter 26

SEVEN MONTHS EARLIER, Chelmsford, Essex

Taylor had lost the argument. She was sitting on the bed sobbing. Her jaw hurt, so did the back of her head where she now had a bump forming. Her hair would hide it of course, but every time she touched it a shooting pain went through her skull. Dennis had never squeezed her face like that before, he usually pulled and twisted the skin on her upper arms but even that had been getting slightly more aggressive each time and was becoming more regular. Usually after he'd been violent he instantly calmed down and was sorry. Not this time though. He still looked just as angry as before. Taylor told him she wasn't going to go to the pub with her workmates.

She couldn't go now even she'd wanted to. Her mascara had run down her cheeks for one thing and there was no way she'd leave Bennie here while Dennis was like this.

Dennis looked at her like she was insane.

"I know you won't! Fucking right you won't! But you wanted to, and the thing with you is-"

As he raised his voice and was almost certainly about to fire out a load more abuse at her, he was interrupted by a loud crying sound. Bennie had woken up.

"It's OK baby go back to sleep." she called out, trying to sound normal.

Dennis' eyes were bulging and he was breathing deeply like a boxer in between rounds. "No fuck that, get up!" Then he stormed into Bennie's room. Taylor followed quickly.

Bennie, slightly whimpering and looking sleepy and confused, got up holding his teddy.

"Bennie go back to bed. It's all OK baby." said Taylor calmly but firmly.

"No it ain't OK. Come here!" snapped Dennis who was almost foaming at the mouth.

Bennie walked over to Dennis.

"You're sick!" she said in disbelief.

"I'm sick?" said Dennis putting his arm around Bennie and pointing at Taylor. "Bennie this is the slut who wants to break up our home and put you in care so she can fuck off with some bloke from her work. This is the nutter who swallowed too much medicine on purpose and had to have her stomach pumped or she'd have died. She wanted to die! That's sick ain't it Ben?"

Bennie burst into hysterical tears.

"Stop it. STOP IT!" screamed Taylor who was now crying herself.

"Oh now *you're* upset? What about me Taylor? What about when I'm upset? You like hurting me but now I know what hurts you don't I?"

Dennis grabbed Bennie's face with his hand, as if he was about to squeeze it exactly as he'd done to Taylor earlier.

"I'm sorry I hurt you Dennis. I'm sorry! I'm sorry! I'm sorry!" she yelled.

"No you're not Taylor! You're just saying it. Saying words. What if I rip his fucking face off? Then you'll be sorry. Proper sorry. Fuck it, I think I will."

Bennie stopped crying. He looked at Taylor with big pleading eyes, went pale and wet himself.

"Get your hands off my son you cunt!" she shouted as she launched herself at Dennis and bit a large chunk out of his face.

Dennis let go of Bennie who ran to Taylor. She hugged him tightly but didn't pick him up. Later she realised that this was probably out of instinct in case Dennis went for her and she dropped him or he got caught in the crossfire.

Dennis had gone completely white. He looked shocked and was holding his face together which was bleeding profusely.

"You nutter. They'll take him off you and put him in care when they see this. You're just like your family."

"Get out of my house!" she screamed in his face.

"I'm going. You're a lunatic. You're scum. I'll report you for this. You'll get sectioned and lose your child. You mad bitch."

If it was his plan to report her he didn't get a chance. Less than twenty-four hours later her and Bennie were knocking on Dave's door with their whole lives neatly packed in suitcases at their feet.

Chapter 27

AS JAMIE CAME BACK with a tray of drinks Natasha looked up from her phone. "How do you say 'home alone' in Spanish?" she asked.

"Ooh I'm learning Spanish!" said Jess excitedly. "Let's see. Home is casa, but you'd say alone home cause the Spanish say it that way. What's the context?"

"Remember that Spanish lad I met Friday night? I'm texting him and we was talking about Christmas films and I wanna say 'Have you seen *Home Alone*?'"

Taylor couldn't believe it. Natasha might as well have just asked what the big yellow thing in the sky was called. "*Home Alone* is a film it's a fucking... Noun! It translates as *Home Alone*!" Taylor was laughing as she said this, and therefore hoped the laughter covered up her shock and outrage.

"No way." said Natasha shaking her head with a smile as if in amazement at the infinite mysteries of the universe.

"Let me see a photo of him." demanded Leah as she grabbed Natasha's phone.

"You met him Friday but you were probably too drunk to remember. You kept calling him Pedro. His name's Paco by the way." explained Natasha.

Leah nodded her approval, "He's nice!" she said, then she held Natasha's phone up to the group so the others could see the photo.

"Oh. He's got a beard. Yuck." said Taylor instinctively. She instantly wished she hadn't said it but couldn't work out why.

"You don't like beards?" asked Jess.

"No. They make me feel sick."

"Thanks a lot." said Jamie.

That's why! Jamie was the only guy she'd ever liked who had a beard, it was a compliment to him in a way that she could see past it, although in a perfect world he'd shave it.

"Sorry. Your beard looks great on you Jamie, but beards in general? No." Not a great recovery there but oh well.

"I like beards, especially Jamie's length. That's the perfect cut off point I think." said Jess thoughtfully.

"Thanks Jess. Anyway, I'm off guys, got work early. See ya tomorrow."

"See you Jamie. I'm just gonna pop to the loo guys." said Jess.

When Jamie left the bar and Jess was in toilet, Leah put her head in her hands and laughed, "Oh my god that was so cringe. *I like your beard Jamie, it's the perfect length.*"

Natasha chuckled then said, "They should get with each other man. They're both such lovely people."

"It won't happen and it wouldn't work." said Leah firmly, like an adult explaining to a child why there'll never be world peace.

"Why not?" asked Taylor curiously, she was very keen to hear the answer to this.

Leah looked at her like she was a complete idiot.

"Because that's not how life works. They're both destined to end up with people who will be horrible to them, treat them like shit and make them miserable."

As Taylor thought about this, Natasha, who didn't even look up from the text she was typing asked, "How do you say 'have you seen *Elf*?'"

Taylor and Leah looked at each other and burst out laughing and for a moment Taylor felt happy and warm and safe. Then she caught a glimpse of herself in the mirror behind the bar. Suddenly she saw quite clearly what the problem was. It was that she was stupid, and she was ugly, and she was mad.

Part 5

IT'S OVER: JESSICA

'And It Just Don't Matter How Hard You Try To Plead, It's All Over, It's Over, It's Over, For Me.'

Chapter 28

"YEAH I'M SERIOUS."

Jess could completely understand why Taylor didn't accept it at face value, for one thing she was lying, but she obviously wasn't doing it convincingly enough. She'd studied drama and she was good at it, she was sure she could convince Taylor that she was being truthful here. She'd just have to try a bit harder.

"Of course I can! I'd love to! But, you know those products are animal tested?"

"Not all though?"

"No, but most."

Taylor really wasn't helping her here.

"Well just give me the makeover and if I like it then don't tell me whether the stuff you've used on me was used to torture innocent living things. I'll just assume I bought the innocent stuff." She said it a bit too quickly she felt, like she was pulling off a plaster. And she might have put too much emphasis on *torture innocent living things*.

But it had worked! Taylor looked delighted. "Brilliant! I'm just going to get a drink. Not being a tight-arse but sticking on my own as it's only a flying visit."

Taylor went to the bar, leaving Jess, Jamie, Leah and Natasha sitting at the table. There was no one else there today except Gloria herself who was behind the bar.

Leah looked Jess up and down with the disgust of a city banker who's just noticed a homeless big issue vender on the doorstep of his favorite Starbucks.

"What the fuck are you playing at? I knew the left were total hypocrites but this is too much."

"I've been single since I've been here, might be time for an image change, that's all."

"Fair play to you man." said Natasha nodding, but Leah clearly wasn't fooled. She grabbed Natasha by the arm.

"Ooh, I'm glad you're here Tasha, I wanted to tell you that I listened to *Unfriended* properly last night and it's actually a really good song."

"Thanks Leah. You really mean it?" asked Natasha looking pleasantly surprised.

"Nope! That was a lie, like Jess just told. I thought we were playing lying." then she smiled at Jess triumphantly.

"Leah, why do you assume she's lying?" asked Jamie, sounding annoyed more than curious.

Jess suddenly felt guilty. Jamie was defending her and here she was lying.

"If Jess was going to get a makeover she'd go to one of those hippy, vegan, everyone wearing sandals, ethical, gay, organic places. She wouldn't use Taylor's bunny Auschwitz stuff. That's how I know." said Leah smugly.

"I do want a makeover but yes you're right Leah. The truth is Taylor's business isn't doing very well at the moment and she's worried. OK?"

She wasn't really fussed on getting a makeover but she added that bit so Jamie wouldn't look silly for defending her.

"You'd do that for her? Wow." said Jamie who was staring at her with a look of shock and admiration.

"I don't like it. But I don't like the idea of her being frightened that she won't be able to feed Bennie even more, so." And that was the long and short of it. If she could just give Taylor money she would but Taylor wasn't the type to accept charity. She was far too proud for that.

"You're an incredible woman Jess."

As Jamie's words entered her ears they flew straight into her heart and instantly turned into butterflies.

"Well it's her own fault if she's skint." Leah remarked, unsympathetically. "Dennis is loaded. Don't know why she doesn't just get back with him."

"Maybe she doesn't want to." snapped Jamie.

"Well she can't moan about being skint then."

"What is it Dennis does for a job?" asked Natasha.

"Property investments. My company generate a lot of the leads. We ask people on the survey 'Would you consider investing in a Spanish property?' If they say yes we sell the info to the brokerage that Dennis works at. I finished top of the office for those leads last two months in a row." Jamie pretty much mumbled this and didn't sound like he was particularly proud of his part in it all.

"Do ya get anything for that?" asked Natasha

Jamie put his head down and looked embarrassed."Yeah. I got a certificate."

Leah looked outraged. "Dennis gets ten percent commission on the deals he does! And they're fifty grand deals. Minimum! Hey Jamie, why don't you show Taylor your certificate? I'm sure that will impress her! Maybe Bennie could eat that? Fucking hell Jamie you don't stand a chance here!"

Jess had absolutely no idea what Leah could possibly have meant by that. "He doesn't stand a chance where?"

"Ignore her Jess." snapped Jamie sounding very annoyed.

"I always do" said Jess, smiling at Jamie and losing herself in his eyes.

Taylor came back with a small glass of coke and rejoined the table.

"I'm free this afternoon Jess. Shall we pop to mine? Dave's bringing Bennie here in a minute then we can go if you like."

Jess wanted to get this over with as quickly as possible. "Brilliant! Ready when you are."

Just then Dennis burst into the bar looking slightly rosy-cheeked (apart from his white jagged scar of course) and he seemed a bit short of breath, almost as if he'd run there. He looked even more cheerful than usual.

"Hi people! I ain't stopping cause I've left my phone in the office so I'd better run back and grab it quick before the boss locks up." Then he just sort of looked at them all. If Dave had been there he would have run over and greeted Dennis of course, but he wasn't, so Dennis just stood there grinning, which was a bit awkward.

"You work Saturdays?" asked Jess. It was something to say.

"Every other Saturday Jessy." Dennis often called people nicknames. He was a flatterer. It didn't work on Jess though. Possibly because, she theorised, you probably had to have a degree of vanity or certainly confidence to believe flattery and Jess had neither. She'd always struggled with receiving compliments even when they appeared genuine. Except for Jamie's which were different and somehow more in context than Dennis'.

Jess also knew that people who could build you up in the way Dennis did, usually had the nasty habit of using the same skill in articulation to knock you down. She could see through Dennis. His flattery wouldn't manipulate her. She could see how it might work on other people though.

"I'm celebrating quickly, I just got a massive deal! One of your leads Jamie! Pop to the bar mate, I wanna buy you a drink to say thanks."

"Jamie tell him about your certificate!" cried Leah, cheerfully.

Jamie ignored her and joined Dennis at the bar.

Chapter 29

"SO, I HEAR THAT'S THE end of your leads? My boss was saying you left your job yesterday cause you've got a job in L.A. We were all a bit gutted mate, your leads were wicked!"

Shit. All Jamie needed right now was Dennis telling everyone. Also he'd go off his biscuits when he found out that Jamie planned to take Taylor and Bennie with him. Jamie felt very awkward to be having this conversation.

It must have shown on his face because Dennis smiled and whispered excitedly, "That lot don't know yet do they?"

"Not yet." A bit of a feeble answer. Maybe he could say he wasn't leaving for a few weeks? Or that he hadn't decided for sure if he was even going yet?

"But you're flying there tonight I heard?"

Bollocks. "Yeah" Jamie said nodding his head and staring into the beer Dennis had bought him.

What excuse could he use now? He couldn't think of a reason why he wouldn't have told them other than the glaringly obvious one. That he was in love with Taylor and he loved Bennie and he planned to surprise them tonight with their tickets. Dennis was bound to be suspicious.

But Dennis didn't look suspicious at all. He looked delighted.

"Fair play to you mate. That's what I'd do. No need for long goodbyes, just fuck off on the flight and email them from the States. Not as if you know them that well is it? I mean, they ain't your *real* mates are they? How long you known them, couple of months? Yeah you're doing the right thing. Don't worry mate, your secret's safe with me. Anyway I've got to run. Good luck in America if I don't see you before you go."

Dennis downed his drink, waved goodbye to the others and ran back out the bar. He seemed so happy that Jamie had genuinely feared that he might hug him or pick him up and spin him around the bar, and was very relieved that he hadn't.

"Jamie did you show him your certif-" began Leah happily as Jamie rejoined the others at the table, but he wasn't in the mood for this so he interrupted her by saying,

"Oh Leah let it fucking go!"

Just then Dave entered the bar with Bennie who was carrying a bear in one hand and a Malaga FC football in the other, both of which Jamie had bought him at the game they went to a week ago. Bennie had named the bear 'Football Bear'. Taylor got up and held her arms out to greet Bennie but he ran straight past her to Jamie and hugged him.

"Hi football boy! Hi Football Bear!" said Jamie.

Taylor looked shocked.

"That's the same bear he's had since last week! He hasn't kept a bear that long for ages." she was smiling more than Jamie had ever seen her smile before, yet she looked like she was going to cry.

"It's Football Bear!" said Bennie to his mother, with authority, like a little sergeant-major, pointing out to one of his corporals something that they should have known in the first place.

"Yeah it is!" confirmed Jamie high fiving both Bennie and Football Bear.

"I just see Dennis, he looked well happy." said Dave.

Shit. Dave must've asked why he was happy and Dennis might have told him that it was because Jamie was pissing off. He'd promised not to of course, but Jamie had an uncomfortable suspicion that Dennis' promises possibly couldn't be relied on.

"He just got a big deal at work." said Natasha and Dave nodded, as if to suggest that she'd cleared up the mystery. That was a relief.

"He's not the only one celebrating work success." said Leah with a smirk. "Tell them about your certificate Jamie!"

Before Jamie could retaliate, Jess slammed her glass down on the table and then her and Leah had their biggest row yet. Jamie wouldn't miss these political debates, they were as futile as two football supporters trying to convince each other that their team is the best. It was pointless and he was glad to think that this was probably the last one he'd have to sit through. As if with this in mind, Leah and Jess made sure they went out on a high, and had the cup final of arguments.

"Leah you think you're so much better than everybody else don't you?"

"Well I usually am!"

"No you're not. It's attitudes like yours that helped usher in the Nazis in Germany."

"Usher was in the Nazis?" asked Natasha looking very confused.

Thankfully Dave clarified the misapprehension. "Nah, you're wrong there Jess. For one thing, Usher's black. He's a brother. And he ain't old enough to have been in the war. He is older than you'd tink ya nah, but he ain't *dat* old!"

"Definitely time to make new friends." said Jamie, accidentally out loud.

"Actually Jess it was attitudes like your 'oh the system's so unfair! Poor little Germans!' Victim complex that caused the holocaust."

"You really are a pathetic little specimen. You're half Indian! Why can't you be proud of that and embrace it? How Natasha does with her Caribbean heritage."

"That's a bit rich. Much like your family! You don't seem very proud of your roots either my aristocratic friend. But you're one of the people aren't you? You think you're so special cause you dress poor and protest against the system and you *hate* capitalism, but how much was your education? More money than most of us have ever seen. You're just as ashamed of your background as I am!"

Leah had obviously hit a nerve. Jess stood up and yelled, "I stand on my own feet and I support myself! I never ask my family or anyone else for help!"

Leah stood up too.

"Yeah because you're a teacher. Because of the qualifications from the university that your family paid for. And for your information, going to slums in India or Cambodia or Uganda on your gap year with a load of posh rich people called Philippa or Cuthbert does not mean you understand poor people. The opposite actually!"

"It must be horrible to be so bitter and full of hate. How many innocent people did Action Five-Sixteen kill because of that venomous hate? Let's see there was the young black footballer. Then there's Natasha's ex-boyfrien-"

Natasha interrupted her by standing up herself with her eyes tightly closed and her fingers in her ears and yelling at them.

"Oh just shut up both of ya! You're both as bad as each other! And you know what? It's fucking boring!

Leah, you see entire communities as scum, and that's really upsetting. My cousin's a solicitor but cause he's Jamaican you'd think he's a criminal. That breaks my heart but Jess you're just as bad! You see entire communities as victims, you think Kane was an innocent victim? Leah's spiteful but you're naive and that's just as fucked up and dangerous. Why can't ya both just see people as people? You know what? Some people *are* scum and some people *are* victims but you won't know who's who unless ya know them. Can't you two talk about something else than this bullshit? You know what? Fuck the pair of you!"

Then she stormed out of the bar in tears.

Leah and Jess both sat down looking a bit shocked.

"Well done Jess! You've just upset a Jamaican. Well, she's a quarter Jamaican. You must be about twenty-five per cent sad right now." said Leah but not in her usual cheerful confident way. Leah's words usually had a bit of swagger about them, they seemed to happily dance out of her mouth as if they were little versions of her and were glad to be used for bullying purposes, but since Natasha's outburst her confidence seemed to have gone and her words sounded flat and lifeless, as if she'd forced them out and they were reluctant to leave her head because it was cold and rainy out there.

"I didn't mean to." said Jess, starting to cry.

Taylor put her arm round her. "It's not really your fault. She seems a bit keyed up at the moment. Think it's all the stuff in the news about the Action Five-Sixteen leader's court case. They keep talking about her ex's murder. It's stressful for her, understandably. She's only twenty and she's never really had a normal life. And they keep saying they're investigating all the A-Five-Sixteen murders but no one's been charged with killing her ex-boyfriend yet and that must be upsetting. Even if they weren't together."

"Yeah that's true Jess. I'm sure she didn't mean to flip at you, she gets upset any time someone mentions her ex." said Jamie,

"Well don't fucking mention him then! Jesus Christ." scowled Leah.

Taylor gave Jess a tissue from her bag and Jess wiped her tears which seemed to mainly be coming from her nose

"I'll go and see if she's OK" she sniffed.

"No. I'll go." said Leah firmly as she got up and left the bar.

Jess was still crying so Jamie put his arm round her and gave her a hug. He didn't like seeing Jess upset. She didn't deserve it as she was such a lovely person.

He was glad it wasn't him who'd upset her. Although thinking about it, he knew that was one thing he didn't need to worry about. He knew for certain that it was massively unlikely he'd ever say or do anything that would make Jess feel sad.

Chapter 30

LEAH HADN'T MEANT TO upset Natasha and add to her stress. She felt bad enough as it was. If she hadn't opened her silly big mouth then Action Five-Sixteen would have killed Kane that night, he'd still be dead, but Natasha wouldn't be a murderer. She felt terrible about that.

There had been a lot of publicity lately about the Action Five-Sixteen murders because of Jason's trial and Leah was worried that Natasha was struggling to cope. She hadn't seemed herself recently and she'd been spending a disproportionate amount of time in the toilet. No one else seemed to have noticed it but Leah had and she was very concerned. The good thing was that Jess was extremely unlikely to come out with any more of her left-wing bile if she knew it would upset Natasha. And if she didn't start it, then Leah wouldn't feel the need to retaliate. She was kind of done with the whole racism thing now. It had been fun while it lasted but it wasn't really her anymore. She was someone else now.

Natasha was sitting in the doorway of a closed down, boarded up bar. She was smoking heroin through tinfoil. Leah approached her unnoticed, she held her phone out and took a perfect photo of Natasha in the act.

"Leah delete that, now!"

"Umm? Nope!"

"Leah I ain't joking fucking delete that photo!"

"I *knew* you were taking drugs again! You need to learn to cope with stress. They won't catch you now you know. You're fine. Stop taking that shit."

"Please delete that photo Leah please. I've paid your fucking rent since you got here. And bought all your drinks."

"And I got you off a murder charge! I'd say that makes us even! Also I didn't kill you! Which I was actually supposed to do." Leah had never told her that before. Although the truth was of course that Leah had *volunteered,* actually *insisted* on killing her so maybe she didn't deserve too much credit for not going through with it.

"I'll pay ya" pleaded Natasha desperately.

"You don't have any money! Plus you shoot blackmailers." Leah felt that was a good point. One thing she'd learned was that you *never* blackmail Natasha.

"I'm serious Leah, I have got money. You know I have. I just wanted to have one group of friends who didn't think I have. Just one group of mates who wanna be my mate and don't expect money for it. So like I said, I'll pay ya."

"You won't have any money if you keep smoking Afghanistan's finest export. Silly!"

"Leah, every friend I've ever had turned out to be a user. Even Kane, who I loved, was using me. I know you ain't a bad person Leah, you like everyone to think that you're bad but I know people, and I know you're a good person, deep down. You're the only true friend I've ever had in my life and I trust you. Leah I know that photo's worth money and I know the papers will buy it off ya but I am *begging* you to promise me you won't send it anywhere."

Leah smiled.

"If you swear to me that you won't take that shit anymore, I'll delete it. Otherwise I'm sending it to your sister Sophie." Natasha stood up and threw the heroin into a bin then sat back down in the doorway.

"Good choice!" said Leah but Natasha looked at her with a serious face, she looked drained.

"Leah I'm gonna give myself up. Look, I obviously aint gonna mention your name or say nothing about you being there that night but I've thought about it and I need to do this."

Was today 'Stop Natasha being an idiot day'? Leah sat in the doorway next to her and put her arm around her.

"He deserved it Tasha. He was blackmailing you about personal stuff wasn't he?" she whispered.

Natasha nodded.

"Yeah" she said, then she nodded again and carried on "He still is though. I shot him so he couldn't blackmail me no more but he still is."

Leah was alarmed. Perhaps Natasha had gone mad and could see Kane's ghost, or maybe she wasn't mad and he was a ghost. He was definitely dead. Leah was sure of that. She'd seen it all of course, Natasha had got him three times, all three had gone into his chest yet when he was lying on the ground he'd had blood trickling out of his mouth, which had surprised Leah at the time.

"What do you mean he's still blackmailing you?" asked Leah, feeling uneasy.

Natasha took a packet of cigarettes out of her pocket, realised the box was empty, scrunched it into a ball and threw it into the gutter whilst making a depressed sounding moaning noise. Leah took a cigarette out of her bag, lit it and passed it to Natasha who didn't thank or even look at her. She took a deep draw, blew the smoke out and said,

"I mean, they're investigating it aint they? They're bound to find out it was me sooner or later. I wake up screaming Leah. I have such bad nightmares now. It just feels like I'm waiting for them to knock at my door and arrest me. If I admit it then that's it, it's over. Kane will be out of my life for good."

Leah took the cigarette out of Natasha's hand, took a drag and gave it back.

"You'll get life Tasha. And you'll be known as a murderer."

Neither of them looked at each other, they both just stared straight ahead.

"I probably won't get that long in jail, they might just charge me with manslaughter. And I wouldn't worry about being a murderer, he weren't exactly very popular was he? If the papers reaction to his death is anything to go by I'll be a hero won't I?"

That was true. Leah couldn't argue with that at all. She probably wouldn't get that long and she would be known as a hero. When she got out there'd probably be book deals and celebrity appearances and maybe a film about it? She might get to play herself or maybe be a consultant on the film set. There was no way Natasha was tough enough to handle prison though, she'd get eaten alive, and probably end up killing herself or having a nervous breakdown but Leah decided it was best to keep that opinion to herself.

"I can't talk you out of this can I?" she asked, not meaning the question to sound quite as rhetorical as it did.

Natasha shook her head. Then she cried. Leah held her and stroked her hair while she sobbed. Natasha pulled herself together after what may have been twenty minutes.

"Thank you Leah" she said meaningfully.

Leah knew what she meant, she meant for everything, but she also meant for not trying to talk her out of confessing. Leah wanted to talk her out of it of course but she could see there was no point, Natasha had made her mind up. When they said goodbye they both acted like it was no big deal, like they'd see each other that night in Gloria's as usual.

"See ya later," said Natasha, unconvincingly, as they went off their separate ways.

Then she flew straight to Luton Airport where she handed herself in to the police and admitted to killing Kane Thomas.

Chapter 31

THE PROBLEM WAS, JESS was a teapot. That was what had led to her getting involved in politics in the first place. But maybe where Leah was concerned, she hadn't been enough of a teapot.

The whole teapot thing had started when she was thirteen. She was the best in her drama class by a mile, she felt, but one day Mr. Scott, her drama teacher, had asked for a volunteer and Jess as usual had put herself forward. Confidently she'd gone up in front of the entire class.

"Jess," Mr. Scott had said in his Birmingham accent, "you're a teapot. And I'm pouring boiling water into you. How does that feel?" he asked, as he tipped an imaginary load of boiling water on her head.

Jess let out an ear-piercing scream. She put her hands over her head in an instinctive, yet futile attempt to stop the imaginary water flow. She imagined it running through her, down her legs and she kicked out her feet manically so as to drain it, she was proud of that bit, it was a good touch she felt. Mr. Scott didn't look impressed though.

"Jess! You're a teapot. A teapot doesn't mind having boiling water poured into it, in fact it rather likes it. You can't just think how *you* would feel. You have to see things from a different point of view."

She'd never forgotten that lesson. And although Mr. Scott had meant it purely as an acting technique, she'd applied it to life and always tried to see things from someone else's point of view. Particularly those who needed it most, the weakest and the disadvantaged, and in doing so she had kind of lost herself, to the point that her wants or desires weren't important or didn't matter anymore. She loved roast beef for example, but she could see it from the cow's point of view and so she became a vegetarian and then vegan. She liked certain clothes but she could see it from the underpaid child worker's perspective and therefore wouldn't purchase them. And then of course there were the cosmetic companies, whose barbaric treatment of animals had stopped her using a lot of beauty products. But she'd decided today that she was going to sort of compromise one of her principles, not by getting the makeover, she'd thought long and hard about that and she'd decided that surely if you avoided animal tested products in order to protect the weakest members of society, and you made one exception in order that a mother could feed her child who may otherwise starve then you weren't in fact compromising your principles at all.

No, what she was going to do which was a kind of principle change was something for herself rather than thinking of anyone else, she was going to do something that would make *her* extremely happy. What would make Jess happy was Jamie.

She hadn't felt this way about anyone since that arsehole Josh and the deeper she fell for Jamie, the more over Josh she felt. Jamie was gorgeous and he was funny and he was ever so sweet and kind, and what he'd said the other week about his dream night in of smoking unfiltered cigarettes and drinking Jack Daniels whilst listening to Frank Sinatra records had really struck a chord and made her yearn to be there next to him, even though she didn't smoke of course, and she didn't like Jack Daniels, but she did like Frank Sinatra music, a bit, some of his songs anyway.

But even without any of that, her and Jamie were quite similar, for one thing they both cared about others. Yes Jess did it on a larger scale involving whole groups while Jamie did on a more localised scale involving individuals, but caring about others is caring about others and it meant they had a lot in common. Jamie was a bit of a teapot too. They could be two little teapots together.

Also, she felt they saw things in a similar way, for instance they both obviously felt Dennis was bad news, and for the same reason, they could both see through him whereas the others maybe couldn't. And of course they both cared about Taylor. Jess loved the way Jamie was with Bennie and how he obviously worried about Taylor and tried to help. Maybe when her and Jamie were a couple they could have a chat and work out some kind of strategy for Taylor, maybe Jamie would know a nice guy who they could set Taylor up with and the four of them could double date! Leah and Natasha wouldn't mind, they seemed to prefer each other's company anyway. They could still all meet up as a group in Gloria's from time to time.

Did Jamie like her in the same way? She thought so, he always laughed at her jokes, and he said lovely things to her sometimes like how he'd said she was incredible for letting Taylor give her a makeover. She didn't want to humiliate herself though, she'd have a chat with him at the first opportunity and test the waters.

Natasha's outburst had really made her think about a lot of things. She'd never meant to upset Natasha and she'd be keeping her political opinions to herself from now on, she was sure Leah would do the same. And hopefully they could draw a line under it. The truth was that Leah really frustrated her. Jess' best friend Poppy (who Natasha had of course correctly identified as bisexual) used to say that if you didn't like someone, it was often because they reminded you of yourself and you saw in them the things you despised about yourself the most. In the case of Leah, Jess had to admit there was probably some truth there.

What Leah had said about her coming from a rich background had really upset her, largely because she'd always been very embarrassed by it. Leah couldn't possibly know the true extent of Jess' family's wealth because Jess had never told anyone but she'd obviously guessed that they were extremely well off. What frustrated her about Leah, she realised, was that Leah had the exact background that Jess would have chosen for herself. She was ethnically diverse, she was strikingly beautiful, and she was from an economically disadvantaged family. And yet, she seemed desperate to be Jess. It was like they'd got mixed up somehow. And while Jess was fighting for ethnic minorities and the under-privileged social class, Leah was fighting for the British elite to stamp down the Union Jack on cultures which they perceived as inferior. They'd both somehow got lost. And as they were both equally embarrassed by their heritage as it contradicted their political viewpoint, they could easily recognise this in each other and therefore knew how to attack the other in their most vulnerable spot, because it was *their own* most vulnerable spot. It was ironic but Leah and Jess actually had a great deal in common and Jess could see that now. She almost laughed as she realised that their greatest rows had been because she was passionately defending Leah's ancestors while with equal passion Leah had been defending Jess'. She made up her mind to tell Leah that, next time she saw her, Leah would probably laugh and that might be a good icebreaker. Maybe they could build a friendship from there.

One of the things that had upset her in the most recent argument hadn't been said by Leah though. It was Jess herself who'd said it. When she said that she'd never asked her family for help. It wasn't true. She had once.

Chapter 32

8 MONTHS AGO, BRISTOL

Jess was sitting on a nice comfy cushion on the floor in the living room. Her and her boyfriend Josh had been renting the house for about three months now. It was a lovely house and they'd really made it a home. She was looking up at Josh who was sitting in a wicker chair playing his guitar. She felt extremely lucky to have Josh, and she was thinking how gorgeous he looked. He was wearing shorts and a V-neck and he had wavy hair and a sexy beard, which complimented his dark brown eyes. Underneath his eye he had a nasty bruise from where he'd been hit with a bottle at the 'Unite Against Fascism' demo last week, but Jess quite liked it, it made him look a bit rugged. He was playing her one of his songs, it was to the tune of *Champagne Supernova* by Oasis but he'd changed the lyrics to a beautiful love song he'd written about the Rwandan genocide. He was so talented. And he sang beautifully...

"So wipe that tear away now from your eye,
cause somewhere in the Congo, walking round the land mines,
there's a Hutu and a Tutsi holding hands,
yeah somewhere in the Congo against the hate, their love shines!
There's a Hutu and a Tutsi,
a Hutu and a Tutsi holding hands."

As he finished he put the guitar down and smiled at her.

"Josh that was so beautiful. I could cry!" She actually nearly had cried.

"It will sound even better when it's properly recorded with backing vocals" Josh said, whilst nonchalantly playing with a statue of a Hindi God which Jess had bought on her gap year in India.

"I'm meeting my mum in an hour. I'm sure she'll lend me the money. I hope you know what a big deal this is, I hate asking her for help".

Josh put the statue back down on the mantel piece.

"I get that. I know it's a mega big thing you're doing. It'll all be worth it though. This album will be huge. I just need it recorded professionally so I can send it to the record companies. We'll pay your mum back then. Every penny."

"We'll pay her quickly I hope. But you're right it is a great album Josh. I'm so lucky to have you. Anyway I'd better get ready. Sing it again for me while I get ready."

He did. And this time she cried.

• • • •

ONE HOUR LATER JESS was in a dainty little tea shop with her mother. Her mother was wearing a cashmere cardigan which did suit her but probably not as much as it had suited the goat who'd almost certainly frozen to death. She was wearing modest yet expensive jewellery and gold-rimmed spectacles. They were sitting at a small table next to a book shelf which was filled with classic literature that was more for decoration than reading.

Jess was trying to stir her tea gently with the tiny silver spoon, as her mother hated the noise of the spoon hitting the china cup and would wince if it happened and look around with embarrassment.

"Yes Mummy it was a bit scary but I had to be there."

"I know you did Jessica. I'm very proud of you. I saw it on the news of course. Those vile Action Five-Sixteen hooligans need to be stood up to. Your father and I are ever so proud but we do worry of course."

Jess felt a twang of annoyance. Her mother was vocally proud of her for opposing the Neo-fascists of Action Five-Sixteen, but why was she so muted when it came to the anti-hunting demonstrations which Jess regularly attended, or the protests against the meat or pharmaceutical corporations? Could it be, Jess would usually wonder aloud, that the Neo-Nazis were working class 'oiks' to use her mother's phrase, whereas the animal torturers were the sort who'd frequent this tea shop? It was infuriating because the obvious class discrimination made Action Five-Sixteen the victims somehow and that wasn't right. If her mother hated them for something they couldn't help, didn't that make her as bad as them? Usually at this point Jess would say all this but, usually she wasn't asking if she could borrow money.

"I understand Mummy. But I was perfectly safe. Although Josh was hit with a bottle when they started throwing things at us."

"Oh dear. Was he injured?"

"Just a little bump on his face. It could have been worse and of course it has been much worse for many of their victims."

"You weren't hit were you?" she asked, looking down the small pair of specks she was wearing as if trying to read Jess' reaction to the question in case she was about to lie. She wasn't, thankfully.

"Only with insults! Apparently I'm 'a posh leftist dyke who needs a good shag from a British cock!' I wouldn't mind having such insults yelled at me but the chap who shouted it had a megaphone! Bit embarrassing."

"It's those imbeciles who should feel embarrassed Jessica, not you."

"Quite. Listen Mummy. I'll cut right to the chase, I wonder if you and Daddy could lend me seventeen thousand pounds?"

Jess was aware that she was speaking far more posh than usual. She was doing it quite consciously. If she didn't she'd usually be told to 'Oh for heaven's sake speak properly Jessica!' and she didn't want to be on the back foot with her mother today. She felt a little devious but knew it was for the best.

"Whatever for?" asked her mother, looking concerned. Jess had never EVER asked her for money before.

"Well you see Josh has such a musical talent Mummy and I really hate to ask but I'd like to pay for him to have his songs professionally recorded. I'll pay you back. Every penny."

Her mother smiled, "Of course we'll lend you the money. I must say he's a very lucky fellow to have you. And your father and I do like him. Tell me, should we expect to have to pay for a wedding soon?"

Josh was the first boyfriend Jess had ever had who her parents actually liked. Although they liked him for different reasons to her of course, Jess liked him for his magnetic, chocolate brown eyes, whereas her parents liked him because his dad banked with Coutts.

"Well I hope so. He hasn't asked me yet of course but, well, I'm rather hoping he will." She was sure he would, and she'd say yes. Yes, yes, yes times a million!

Her mother adjusted her specks and reached into her handbag, "And if that's what you want then so am I. Now, who do I make this cheque out to?"

Chapter 33

SIX DAYS LATER THE house didn't look a home anymore. Not her home anyway. It was amazing what a difference moving one person's things out made. It wasn't just the space it created which made the house appear bigger, it was more that it completely changed the personality of the house somehow.

All her things were in suitcases. She saw the photo on the mantelpiece of her and Josh on their skiing holiday. It looked quite conspicuous now, with all her artifacts which had been surrounding it gone. She loved that photo. Why should he have it?

She picked it up and looked at it then she started to cry.

"How could you? After I went to my mother for money? How could you?" She was looking at the photo of Josh as she asked this but real Josh answered her.

"Jess I'm so sorry. It just happened."

Something about his body language was wrong but Jess couldn't quite put her finger on it.

"I came to the studio to tell you I was so proud of you. To catch you and her doing that!"

"It will never happen again Jess. From now on she's just my backing singer and nothing else."

She couldn't believe what she'd just heard. "You're not serious? You still want *her* as your singer!"

"She's got a great voice and-" he started to say but Jess interrupted him.

"I really suggest you don't finish that sentence. I'm leaving now Josh."

"Jessica I'm sorry. She spun my head a bit, I plan to marry you, you know, I just felt I need to get some things out of my system first and she was one of them."

And then Jess saw with dreadful clarity, exactly why Josh had done what he'd done. She could see it in his eyes.

"You're not sorry are you? You're glad you got caught. This relationship was getting a little too serious for you wasn't it Josh?"

"Don't be so silly! I still want to be with you. But you're right to leave. I think you need time to calm down and forgive me. Call me when you've found it in your heart to forgive me Jess."

Jess packed the photo in her case. Six hours later when she landed at Malaga airport she took it out of her bag with the sole intention of throwing it in a rubbish bin but she couldn't, she wasn't ready yet, she'd had that photo ever since.

Chapter 34

"SO WE'LL ALL MEET HERE at eight? Taylor? You and Bennie will both be here right?" Jamie sounded a bit agitated.

"Yeah, I'm giving Jess a makeover then we're coming back here. We'll be here about seven. What's the panic?" asked Taylor.

"Just arranging the night. No panic. So you and Bennie will be here. Phew."

He didn't ask Jess if she'd be there.

He was probably just about to though when Bennie grabbed him and said, "You're captain poo poo!"

Jamie did a pretend outraged face.

"Oh yeah? Well, captain poo poo's gonna get ya!" Then he chased Bennie out of the bar. Bennie held his bear and squealed with joy as he ran outside.

Jess decided now might be a good time to lay the groundwork.

"I'm gonna see if he catches him. I'll meet you at yours in an hour Taylor."

Jess walked out of the bar and almost bumped straight into Dennis who was coming in.

"Oops, sorry Dennis. I Almost fell on top of you!" she said, apologetically.

"Now there's a dream I've had a few times." said Dennis with a cheeky wink as he walked into the bar.

Jess walked over to Jamie who was having a cigarette and kicking the football back and forth with Bennie.

"God he's a creep!" she said looking back towards the door where Dennis had just walked.

"Yep." said Jamie, nodding his head

"I'd say we're the only ones who don't like him?"

"Yep."

"But we're best not to say anything. If you don't like someone you should really keep that to yourself."

"I agree."

"But if you *do* like someone you should tell them shouldn't you?"

"I'd say so." said Jamie distractedly as he pretended to boot the ball hard but stopped short and gently lifted it towards Bennie with his foot instead, the ball went over Bennie's head and he ran after it laughing.

Jess took a deep breath.

"I mean, if you hang around in a group of friends but you are absolutely crazy about someone in that group you should tell them? Right?" It was out there now. She smiled at him and searched his face for a reaction.

He turned and looked at her a bit suspiciously, then he grinned a lovely beaming smile, he looked a little bit nervous, but Jess was feeling quite nervous too of course.

"I see what you mean Jess. Yes. I think you should."

"Even if that could wreck a lovely friendship?" she asked inquisitively. This was important because her and Jamie did have a lovely friendship.

"If it could be so much more then, yeah, it's worth the gamble. That's what I think."

"That's exactly what I think too. I'm going to Taylor's now. I'll see you tonight Jamie."

Jamie smiled back at her.

"Yeah see you tonight Jess."

YES! This was going to be the start of something amazing. She couldn't really say much more to him now as the setting wasn't right not with Bennie and everything. But she'd said enough and more importantly *heard* enough to know that she wasn't about to embarrass herself or end up disappointed here. She'd tell him exactly how she felt tonight. She had a good idea how to.

Chapter 35

TAYLOR WAS JUST FINISHING her drink ready to leave the bar to do Jess' makeover. She sipped at it slowly as she wanted to let Bennie have a little while playing with Jamie, she knew how much he loved that. She was thinking about how things were starting to go OK for them for once when Dennis walked in.

"Taylor can I ask you something? About the time you took the overdose?"

"Jesus Dennis".

She looked around with a sense of dread but luckily no one had heard him, Jess, Jamie and Bennie were outside and Leah had of course gone looking for Natasha who'd stormed off so it was just them left in the bar, except Gloria who was unloading some glasses from the dishwasher and she didn't seem to have heard. Why was he bringing this of all things up now?

"Hear me out. You didn't really want to die did you? It was just a cry for help. Not that you're an attention seeker. Just that, everything was slipping away, and you were scared, and you were losing control, and you didn't know what else to do. You were out of options."

"Can we please not talk about this?"

"The question I wanted to ask is, do you think you'll ever do that again?"

He asked it like he was conducting a market research questionnaire. Maybe he'd worked out that she would never get back with him and he wanted her to top herself, perhaps he was going to suggest it and then hand her a box of pills and a plastic bag.

"What a stupid question. Of course I won't."

"I know you won't. Taylor that night, when you left, how I acted, I'd never EVER do that again either. I wouldn't have hurt Bennie. Not really. I was just terrified cause I felt I was losing you. I love you. Both of you."

"Dennis you were violent to me loads of times. It wasn't a one off. That was just the only time you turned on Bennie. He hasn't been the same since that night, I can't forgive you for that Dennis. I can't. And I won't." she said it very firmly, and as the words left her lips, she realised how much she meant them.

"I don't expect you to. Not yet anyway. I'll make it up to you both. I love you so much Taylor and this can be a new start for us. I'm making a fortune out here and I just wanna take care of you both, we can send him to the best private schools. Give him a real chance you know? You'd never take an overdose again and I'd never hurt or threaten to hurt either of you again. Everyone makes mistakes Taylor. You've made yours and you're not the same person you were when you tried to take your own life. And I'm not the same person I was that horrible night. I love you. So much. We could have an incredible life together. The three of us."

"Bennie's just starting to settle again Dennis. And we've got a nice group of friends out here. I'm glad you're sorry but as for me and you? Getting back together? That won't be happening."

"I know. They're a great bunch. And we can stay here. I know Bennie's settled and I know you guys are both fond of Jamie and it'll be upsetting for you when he leaves but I'm sure he'll write to you guys and we can make a great life out here."

What the fuck?

"When he leaves?"

"Shit. I promised him I wouldn't say anything. He's moving to California, tonight. I told him to tell you. I said that you're his best mate out here and that Bennie's really attached to him and he owes you both a proper goodbye but he said you ain't his real mates, he's only known you both a couple of months and he'd rather just slip away. He don't do goodbyes he said."

"That's a lie. You're lying Dennis." He had to be. He just had to be.

"Ok. I'll take a bet with you if you like? I'll give you a thousand to one odds that he's not here tomorrow. Please don't say nothing to him though Tay. I promised him. I'm sorry. I know he meant a lot to you. You're one of life's amazing people and you care about others and their feelings. He isn't."

Taylor ignored this and walked over to Gloria. She could feel her heart beating and her mouth felt dry, her legs were shaking. *Calm down Taylor, this is clearly nonsense* she told herself.

"Gloria. Is Jamie moving to America? Tonight?"

Taylor knew. She looked in Gloria's face and she knew. And her heart cracked.

"Um. I don't know." said Gloria finally, looking extremely uncomfortable.

"You don't know? You don't know if your own cousin's emigrating tonight or not?"

"Taylor. It's not really my place to say, um, how did you find this out?"

"Does that matter? He's leaving. I can't believe this. I thought... I thought maybe that... Maybe we might... I thought...how can he not tell me?"

"I'm sure he's going to." said Gloria smiling. Taylor felt the smile was inappropriate, and what Gloria had just said was a stupid thing to say.

"What the day he leaves! After building such a lovely relationship with Bennie he can just walk out of his life like that? He never cared about us did he? Not the way I... Not really."

Gloria looked panicked. "Taylor you've got this wrong it's not what you-"

She didn't get to finish whatever she was about to say as Dennis yelled over and interrupted her. But Taylor didn't really want to hear it anyway.

"Taylor I'll go and grab Bennie then maybe take you guys for lunch quickly before you give Jess her makeover? My treat. We can have a chat yeah?"

Taylor looked at the floor. How could she have got this so wrong? She knew she was stupid but she didn't realise she was *that* stupid. Everything she'd thought, about their bond, about their connection, about their future even, it was all rubbish. It was in her head, she'd made it all up. She must've done if he was just going to fuck off to America like that without so much as a goodbye. She just wasn't one of life's winners. She wasn't tough or smart enough to understand things. She didn't have her mum's toughness at all. She was sure Dennis wasn't capable of change and that her and Bennie should get as far away from him as possible. But she'd been sure about Jamie too. She obviously wasn't a good judge of character. What if Dennis was right about Bennie going to the best schools and things? She could end up holding him back and ruining his life with her bad decisions, and that wasn't fair on him. She couldn't let her madness screw his life up. Dennis had actually never hurt Bennie, had she overreacted? She was a nutter after all. She felt weak and tired and incapable of making her own decisions.

"OK." she said softly

Dennis smiled and left the bar to get Bennie.

As Taylor got her bag Gloria grabbed her by the arm.

"Listen Taylor" she said urgently, but Taylor didn't let her finish as whatever excuse she was going to make for her cousin wasn't going to change the facts.

"I'm not in the mood to talk right now Gloria. I really just cannot believe this."

As Taylor walked out of the bar to Dennis who was waiting by the door with Bennie, Gloria got her phone out and began to text Taylor: *'u got this all wrong. He loves u and Bennie, he's going 2 ask'*... But at this point Jamie walked back in the bar and Gloria quickly put the phone down.

Chapter 36

JAMIE HAD NO IDEA HOW the hell Jess knew that he was going to tell Taylor that he was in love with her. Gloria must have told her he supposed. It didn't matter though, she obviously thought it was the right thing to do, she'd said as much. She said if you hang around in a group but you're crazy about someone in that group you should tell them, and she was right of course. She was great Jess. He was just finishing his cigarette when Dennis came out the bar and took Bennie, followed by Taylor and the three of them walked off. She didn't even look at him. Almost as if she didn't want to but he wasn't worried. She was always keyed up when Dennis was around and anyway, he'd see her later of course. He'd tell her then, he'd tell her how he loved everything about her, her sexy tough look, her ocean blue eyes, how she was with Bennie, her humorous way of looking at the world. Everything.

The main thing he wanted to say to her was of course obvious, and she must see it every time she saw her reflection in a mirror. He'd tell her anyway, but she must already know how she was intelligent and she was beautiful and she was perfect.

He walked back into the bar and smiled at Gloria. "Gloria? Did you tell someone about what I'm doing?"

"Jamie I didn't tell her! She already knew!" Gloria sounded really flustered.

"Dennis must've let something slip about me leaving and she's worked out what I'm gonna do. Oh well no harm done."

"What?" asked Gloria, looking at him like he was crazy.

"She thinks it's a good idea and I should do it."

"She said that?"

"Yeah! She said it's worth risking a good friendship if it could be something more. Don't look so worried cuz. It's all good. I'll see you later." He hadn't meant to make Gloria worried. He wasn't really bothered if she'd told Jess.

As Jamie left the bar Gloria was confused but very relieved. She deleted the message to Taylor without sending it.

Chapter 37

FOUR HOURS LATER TAYLOR was in Gloria's bar with Dennis and Dave. Dave was of course delighted that they were back together. She'd explained to him that it was very early days and they were taking things slowly but he'd still insisted on buying them some of Gloria's cheap champagne. As Dennis put his arm around her and leaned in to kiss her she thought she saw Jamie out the corner of her eye outside the bar, but she couldn't have done, because when she looked back there was nobody there.

Chapter 38

TROJAN HORSE
'You don't need to break my walls, you just creep inside unknown.'

• • • •

JAMIE HAD BEEN NERVOUS as he sat in the barber's chair. He didn't like being clean-shaven as he was sure that it made him look about twelve but he knew that Taylor hated beards. As the barber shaved his beard off, he looked at the three tickets to the USA in his hand, in his, Taylor and Bennie's names and smiled to himself. He realised something quite important. Taylor was the first woman he'd ever liked *and* fancied. It was usually one or the other. Yet he was looking forward to snuggling up with her and playing board games or chatting on the plane or exploring California with her just as much as he was looking forward to the other thing they'd hopefully do. Now he thought about it, that was what love was, exactly that. Thinking about the dirtiest things and the cleanest things yet picturing the same person in both scenarios. If he had to choose the perfect woman on looks alone it would be Taylor, every time. But if he had to choose the perfect woman based on everything but looks it would be Taylor as well. He knew he was doing the right thing here.

• • • •

TAYLOR HAD SEEMED VERY distracted as she gave Jess her makeover and Jess was concerned. As she walked from Taylor's house to the tobacco shop, a load of guys who were working on a building site were wolf whistling someone and shouting 'guapa' which Jess knew was Spanish for beautiful but she had no idea who they were yelling at because she couldn't see anyone else on the street.

She was just about to cross the road when a car driven by a young Spanish guy drove passed her and hooted, she looked around to see if she'd dropped something but she hadn`t. Why had he hooted at her? Maybe he thought she was about to cross in front of him.

She'd never been in a tobacco shop before because she'd quit smoking long before she moved to Spain but she was pleasantly surprised by the shop. There were two guys in front of her in the queue yet they politely insisted that she go in front of them and the two guys behind the counter almost fought each other to serve her! They must have been on commission.

She bought a packet of unfiltered Camel which were the only unfiltered brand available and put them in the bag she was carrying. Inside the bag was a vintage edition bottle of Jack Daniel's which had cost her most of her wages and a vinyl *Come fly with me* Frank Sinatra record on which she'd stuck a little note which read, 'Thought we could have that Frank Sinatra night together x'.

She didn't like giving the tobacco companies her money, and in all honesty she didn't like giving her money to Jack Daniel's either, considering it was actually invented by a former slave who had received none of the credit for it and still less any of the profits. But she was compromising on her usually rigid principles because she kept imagining Jamie's face on their Sinatra night and she wanted him to be happy. She was changing, she felt. Then she took the photo of herself and Josh out of her handbag, and looked at it. She was finally ready, she threw it in a bin and walked round the corner to Gloria's bar.

• • • •

JAMIE COULDN'T BELIEVE his eyes as he looked into Gloria's bar from the street. He walked off, ripping Taylor and Bennie's flight tickets up and threw them in the gutter. He got into a taxi, and just said the word 'airport'. The taxi sped off.

• • • •

JESSICA WALKED ROUND the corner to Gloria's. She saw Jamie ripping something up and storming off looking devastated and looked through the window of Gloria's to see what had upset him. Taylor was back with Dennis! It was obvious from how they were sitting, he had his arm around her and he looked delighted with himself. Taylor didn't look happy though. Was that why she'd seemed so distracted and disengaged earlier?

No wonder Jamie was upset, like Jess he thought the world of Taylor and... then it hit her. Jess had a horrible feeling in the pit of her stomach. Suddenly everything made sense. Him saying about how you should tell someone in your group of friends if you had feelings for them, his hatred of Dennis, his concern for Taylor and Bennie, his and Taylor's wine and board games night, Leah saying how Jamie didn't stand a chance and Jess not knowing what she'd meant.

It was amazing how much you remembered when you realised you'd been an idiot. It was all playing in her head like a flashback. As he'd just stormed off there was something different about him. What was it? He was clean-shaven. Why? *Because Taylor had said that she hated beards.* He'd gone to all that effort just for Taylor.

Jess looked down at the bag she was carrying with the Sinatra record, Jack Daniel's and cigarettes. She had been right. Her and Jamie did have a lot in common. He didn't see her as she put her head down, turned around, and walked back the way she came.

An hour later as she was sat on a curb, swigging from the Jack Daniel's bottle and smoking an unfiltered cigarette she realised she hadn't changed at all and she hadn't learned anything from the Josh experience. She'd got it all wrong again. She was a shit teapot. She took a deep drag of the cigarette, winced and pulled the stray bits of tobacco from her mouth. She actually felt sorry for Jamie, and herself of course and Taylor and Bennie too if Dennis was anything like she suspected he was. Her heart was broken in quite a few places.

• • • •

NO ONE CAME INTO THE bar that night. Not Jess, not Jamie, not Leah or Natasha. Just her, Bennie, Dave and Dennis.

Taylor needed a minute alone. She meekly excused herself from the table and walked into the toilet. She was so deep in her own head that she didn't notice that Bennie had followed her. She stood by the sink staring at herself in the mirror. Then she burst into tears. It felt as though her reflection started crying before she did.

Suddenly she realised Bennie had wondered in after her and was stood at her side. He put his hand on her and was looking up at her concerned and frightened so she quickly wiped away her tears and smiled at him. But he didn't smile back. Instead he handed her 'Football Bear' to operate on. As she opened up the bear she remembered how calm, happy and content he'd been when Jamie had bought him that teddy.

She looked at Bennie, he was looking up at her with big, pleading eyes. Then she looked down. She didn't need to look because she already knew, it was mother's instinct, but she looked anyway. Her heart completely shattered. Bennie had wet himself.

• • • •

THE DETECTIVES WHO were investigating Kane's murder were quite nice to her considering. They pretty much insisted that she get legal representation and the appointed solicitor explained to her that although she was or had been famous and there'd been less than complimentary things said about her in some newspapers, a jury would be instructed to put that out of their minds if there was a trial. However, since she was admitting killing Kane he felt she'd probably just be charged with manslaughter. There probably wouldn't be a trial at all. But the detectives, understandably, had some questions for her.

"Why did you shoot him?" asked the main one. He was Scottish and aged about forty five and had a bald head and a moustache.

She looked him straight in the eye "He was blackmailing me."

"What was he blackmailing you about?"

"He knew stuff. Personal stuff, I'm not going to say what it was."

The other detective who hadn't asked her any questions yet was probably in his thirties and had spiky hair and stubble. He explained to her that she didn't have to answer the question but it might help her if they knew what she was being blackmailed with. Also, that it may harm her defence if she didn't tell them now but did attempt to use it as part of her defence in court. Then the main one asked her if she'd like to elaborate on what the blackmail was.

"No" She said firmly, looking at the wall.

"Let's move on. Where did you get the gun?"

"It was his gun. He was forcing me to carry it for him."

"Where is it now?"

"Gone. I threw it in the river."

"Well at least it's off the streets. You've solved a mystery for us I can tell you. Ballistics confirmed that firearm had been used in some pretty vicious yardie related crimes, all of which Kane Thomas was suspected of. You can imagine the confusion that created. It did seem unlikely that he'd topped himself then made the gun disappear." Then the two police officers looked at each other as if they were trying not to smile, she got the impression they didn't like Kane very much.

Then they asked her to explain in her own words exactly what had happened. She explained that she'd pointed the gun at him in order to scare him into leaving her alone but he'd advanced on her and she'd instinctively fired at him three times at which point he'd dropped to the ground.

"Are there any witnesses to this?"

"No." she lied.

Did she have any idea why the National Retaliation Force had claimed responsibility for the attack only minutes later? This flustered her a bit. "I..um.. I did that. I was panicking and I thought if I did that I might not get arrested. I acted on instinct. I must have been in shock."

"So just to be clear, it wasn't a racially motivated attack?"

"Of course not. I'm mixed raced myself."

The two detectives seemed satisfied by this. She felt sure this was coming to a close.

"Just one more question. This was the only NRF attack which was claimed by a woman and that information was never released to the press so again, you've cleared up a mystery but, what's puzzling me is, the codeword given was authentic, it was a genuine code which the NRF use to claim attacks. How could you possibly have known it?"

"Because I was the spokeswoman for Action Five-Sixteen silly!" said Leah, smirking at the stupid policeman.

This was great fun! Most people go to prison because the police have outsmarted them, she was going because she'd outsmarted the police. She wouldn't get that long. These idiot coppers were believing every word she said. She was thoroughly enjoying herself.

Natasha would see on the news or whatever that Leah had handed herself in, then she could stop worrying, she wouldn't have been able to handle prison, Leah would handle it though, she was quite looking forward to it.

Being a right-wing activist had been really great fun, being an expat had been a total disappointment, it was boring and depressing and quite lonely. It was time to try something new. Being a jailbird might be fun, at least it would be a new adventure.

Leah had always enjoyed TV shows about prisons, *Orange Is The New Black, Oz,* the other one she couldn't remember the name of... *Bad Girls!* That was it!

She smiled. She'd be OK.

Don't miss out!

Click the button below and you can sign up to receive emails whenever Gus Duffy publishes a new book. There's no charge and no obligation.

https://books2read.com/r/B-A-JYAG-OYJS

BOOKS 2 READ

Connecting independent readers to independent writers.

About the Author

Gus Duffy grew up in Harrow, North West London and currently resides on the Costa Del Sol, Southern Spain.

A little bit of the moon is his debut novel.

Printed in Great Britain
by Amazon